The Rebellion of Esmeralda

The Rebellion of Esmeralda

Mark Scarpaci

Writers Club Press
San Jose New York Lincoln Shanghai

The Rebellion of Esmeralda

All Rights Reserved © 2000 by Mark Scarpaci

No part of this book may be reproduced or transmitted in any form or by any means, graphic, electronic, or mechanical, including photocopying, recording, taping, or by any information storage retrieval system, without the permission in writing from the publisher.

Writers Club Press
an imprint of iUniverse.com, Inc.

For information address:
iUniverse.com, Inc.
5220 S 16th, Ste. 200
Lincoln, NE 68512
www.iuniverse.com

ISBN: 0-595-13842-X

Printed in the United States of America

To Chuck and Betty Scarpaci

Acknowledgements

Thanks to Carolann and Bus Clough for sharing their "Mexican" secret. To all my friends and supporters at Tektronix, especially Jerry Schneider and Laura Whitaker. Annie Seabrook deserves a medal for plowing through the huge first draft. Elizabeth Lyon's expert editing suggestions paved the way. And a special thank you to my wife Kari Jorgensen, for being patient, kind and understanding of the process.

Prologue

Martin Slate opened the huge white gate and entered the compound greeted by a gentle ocean breeze. His head cleared a little, his body felt strong. He didn't feel drunk, just cleansed. He walked over to the terrace and looked down at the lagoon. Turquoise blue water gently lapped the white sand beaches. Coconut trees swayed in the rhythm of the air.

How many times in the last twenty years had Martin Slate leaned back in his chair at work and fantasized about going to an Island paradise? He recalled his usual daydreams…

I threaten to quit my job if they don't give me a year's leave. They give in. A couple of plane rides later and I'm on a tropical island. A soft, warm breeze blows down a lonely white sand beach. The first touch of the water tells me it's eighty-degrees. A beautiful native woman in a white dress hands me an exotic drink and a warm lunch for the equivalent of one American dollar. No phones. No cubicles. No power lunches or boring all day corporate meetings that make me grind my teeth at night. Just the soft sound of waves crashing on the shore. While napping in a hammock I invent a new piece of computer hardware that gets rave reviews. The headlines read, "Ex-Tektronix engineer breaks new creative ground. Intel and Microsoft knocking at his door."

The sweet ocean breeze blew on Martin's face, snapping him out of his revelry. He took the invitation and entered the warm water with a surfboard. He paddled out past the edges of the lagoon, lay his head down on the board and promptly passed out. He dreamt of a land where there were no divorce, no car crashes, no "downsizing", just strong palm frond furniture and Gorde's mix of tequila and Sangrita.

When Martin awoke his back was burnt bright red and it was late. He rolled over, scratched the gray hair on his chest and thought about the huge hunk of dough he had in mutual funds in the United States. None of it really mattered to him now.

He saw the shore wasn't more than a few hundred yards away, and started to paddle in. By the time he reached the bay it was nearly dark. The waves seemed bigger, breaking on a reef he hadn't noticed before. Martin tried hard to avoid the waves but a huge curl picked up his board and threw him over into deep water. He managed to hold his breath while being thrashed about, although for a moment he couldn't tell which way was up. Finally, he managed to get his head to the surface, take a breath and suck…he was carried up by another huge wave and slammed onto a beach of coarse black sand. Martin's skin was raw, his head hurt and to make matters even worse, he realized now that he wasn't even on his beach. His beach had white sand.

No huts in sight. No stairs. No nada. He tried to get up but his body wouldn't respond. He wasn't sure if it was the thrashing he'd just taken or Gorde's mixture of spirits and chilies.

He waited, took a few deep breaths and tried again. "No luck big boy," he whispered to himself. "Maybe that son of a bitches mixture of tequila and chilies really has worked its magic and I'll be paralyzed for life," he mumbled.

Martin dug around a bit, made a crude sand pillow and prepared for a night on the beach. As he lay his head down on the pillow he saw a small white object that startled him. After he realized it moved rather slowly, he took a better look. It looked like an egg, but it moved. A few more seconds passed and the egg stopped moving but a small, dark green object slowly crawled right at him. It was a small turtle, not more than the size of a silver dollar. Just a little bitty turtle that was about to change his life, once and for all…forever.

Chapter 1

Ferdinando Gaupaulaupe Ramirez, simply known as Nando to his friends, stood high above his black sand beach and gazed down at a lobster-red speck shimmering against the black sand. He hadn't noticed it the day before—probably a dead turtle part, he thought. Poachers still came through his waters every couple of years, trying to find his turtle's home. Luckily, they had never been successful, although every now and again they caught up with one of the adults in the open ocean and killed them for eggs.

He decided to do his daily dance, then go down to explore.

Nando didn't look a day over sixty-five. At one-hundred-and-thirty-one years old, he was a living part of the ancient folklore. Born on the island in a small village named Hermana, Nando believed that if you followed your instincts and pursued your life's work, you'd live a long and healthy life. Nando believed that for every minute you worked on your labor of love you'd gain a minute of youthful health and vitality. His love was turtles.

Maybe his obsession was a holdover from the ancient Zapoteca cultures of 900 to 1500 AC, or maybe Nando just naturally took to these huge marine reptiles. Whatever the case, Nando knew all there was to know about his reptilian friends.

For years he had watched the females drag their huge bodies up on shore, dig holes about a foot deep and deposit close to eighty round, almost chicken-sized eggs into the nest. Most sea turtle eggs were the size of ping-pong balls with an outer shell the consistency of a soft-shell crab, so these were huge.

About fifty-five days later "los ninos," as he referred to them, would burst out of the nest and roam to the sea. Unfortunately, only one or two of the eighty would survive to become adults. It was nature's struggle.

Nando himself stood five foot two and weighed ninety-seven pounds and possessed the flexibility of an Olympic gymnast. He could curl his body around a pole like a snake, using it to climb up a palm tree to extract coconuts. Or, he could put his legs behind his head and turn into a human bowling ball, rolling down his hill through the soft dirt and landing in the deep sand, slowing down just in time to unravel before hitting the roaring Pacific. He did this type of acrobatic roll nearly every day of his adult life on his way out to swim.

He swam like a dolphin, coming in and out of the water with his flipping, contorting body. He'd usually go out for an hour or so, sometimes taking an extended swim that could last up to three hours. On his long swims, if he got tired, he'd find one of his beloved sea turtles heading in the right direction and latch on to its shell. Nando would hold on for dear life, flapping like a flag in the breeze, the turtle carrying him closer to his beach—the only black sand beach on the island.

His mind, although not educated in the traditional ways of the world, had a memory like a Pentium Plus computer. He knew one thousand and one hundred and eighty-five different songs and dances by heart, and sang a different song, along with a different dance, for every day of his year, which, coincidentally, was one thousand one hundred and eighty-five days long.

Singing was a custom he had learned as a child, when he would watch his Grandfather and Father put on their painted masks and dance—enjoying every step, ("like breathing air itself" his *Abuelito* used to say). They'd dance their morning movements, joyously singing, with one of them usually accompanying the other with a drum or a flute.

Now, when he was dancing, many times he felt like his Grandfather and Father were right there in the room with him. He could hear them playing along with a flute or a drum, kicking up dust, laughing, singing and enjoying themselves.

For Nando, it also wasn't a strange occurrence to be his age and so vital and healthy.

Many of the people in Hermana had lived to be one hundred and thirty, even one hundred and forty years of age, and usually stayed fit and lucid until the day they realized life was pretty much over. Then, they would gather around all their friends, have one final fiesta and, with a farewell wave, walk into the mountains and go to the other side. Of course, with the longevity of the people, this didn't always work as planned.

Nando remembered over eighty years ago when Paublito Aberanca, one of the last men who broke the age barrier of one hundred and forty, reached the ripe old age of one hundred and thirty seven. Paublito was still fit, not really ready to go, but when he caught a bad cold in his late one hundred and thirties, he figured it was time. So he walked up the hill thinking his time was up and instead, came back to the village four days later with a new wife, Bettita Mendino. Bettita, herself one hundred and twenty-three, had taken her last walk into the mountains just days before and had been sitting under a tree waiting for the hand of death to come take her away.

"Paublito's hand was a lot more appealing," Bettita joked to her sister on her wedding day. "And besides, I was too young to go up the hill!" But the likes of Paublito Aberanca, Bettita Mendino and others who lived far into their hundred's were vanished now, gone for many a year.

Their demise had been sudden and rapid. Back in the early 1950's, years after Nando had left Hermana for his beach side retreat to care for his turtle's breeding grounds, a tragic pestilence hit Hermana. It was worse than the flu that had killed off many of the mainlanders when the Spanish had arrived. Worse than the plague that had swept Europe. It was something so profound, so sneaky in its attack, that before anyone knew what had happened, the whole village had lost its traditional will to live. It…was the peso.

The whole idea of working for money, rather than working for life, was so far removed from their existence, that when the peso arrived, and slowly wormed its way into their culture, the damage was done, before anyone had known.

It turned the village into a rotting coconut, eaten from the inside out, with only a paper thin shell holding it all together. When the veneer of Hermana cracked, the longevity of the people of Hermana disappeared. Nando, removed from the infectious disease, was the only survivor of days gone by, where you worked for life and not for a living.

In the village of Esmeralda, there were many theories as to why Nando had outlived his whole family. Some thought it was his clean living, daily exercise and mental stimulation. A few others, old enough to remember the old ways, believed that Nando was following his life long love of turtles to his life rather than to his grave.

Whatever the case, most everyone who knew about Nando (most of them had passed away) agreed that he should be left alone on his remote stretch of beach called Black Sands, to finish up his life in peace and quiet. They thought he was like the last surviving member of a sacred yet quickly dying breed of animal living out its final days in the zoo.

In fact, Nando was the shepherd of such an animal. The Emerald Belly turtles, which once roamed over a thousand mile stretch of beach, now only resided on the island of Esmeralda. Approximately two hundred females and five hundred males remained and they looked so much like the standard Leatherback, people didn't realize there was a difference.

So Ferdinando Gaupaulaupe Ramirez, or Nando, at one hundred thirty-one years of age, stood in his cliff top cave, high above the black sand beach, doing his daily dance. Suddenly he saw Martin, the small red speck, get up from the sand and turn into a tall red man who stumbled along the beach. One side of him was the color of the inside of a coconut, the other side, the bright red color of Himica, Nando's favorite drink made from wild flowers.

Nando quickly found his most fierce looking mask (eyes painted red and black with white protruding horns and yellowish/green spots dappling the throat and neck area), and painted a few broad white stripes across his chest. He wanted to scare this man, and scare him good, keep him away from los ninos. He didn't want to kill him. But he would, if he had to. He would do just about anything to protect his turtles.

He grabbed his smaller machete, straightened up his mask, tucked into a ball and let himself roll down the soft dirt trail. Within a few seconds he had traveled down the two hundred-foot cliff. Letting the deeper sand slow him down, he landed about ten feet in front of the big red man, unfolded from his human bowling ball position and stood up. He dusted off his body, straightened his mask and pulled his machete from his waistband—ready for war.

Martin Slate, however, wasn't. Initially startled when he saw the Indian arrive, Martin turned to meet Nando, but then, slowly, as if he were running out of the very energy needed to stand, he melted down to the sand and sadly looked up at the diminutive masked man in silence.

Nando looked around for the man's boat. Nothing. He took one look into Martin's eyes and knew this one wasn't here to take eggs or kill turtles. This man was in trouble…or troubled.

It had been a long time since anyone had come to his secluded beach without the express motive of hunting his turtles or stealing their eggs, not since another blond-haired surfer had arrived so many years ago. Nando had helped the other surfer and he would do the same for this one.

He ran back up to his hut and returned with water and food. He dabbed Martin's forehead with water and fed him a little pineapple. He left the food and went back to his hut, sewing together coffee bags to make a protective canopy. He covered the still silent Martin with it. Nando then found the surfboard, patched it up, and brought it back down to the beach.

"Thank you," Martin mumbled. But Nando didn't understand the words. He gave Martin more pineapple and Martin tried to stand up again, only to collapse. Finally, Nando managed to put Martin back on the repaired surfboard, covering his red skin with the light canvas cover and swam him out into the current. He knew this current would deposit Martin on the Esmeralda side of the island.

Martin looked back, afraid he was being pushed to his death, then passed out with the blurry image of the little Indian swimming through the ocean like a dolphin.

Chapter 2

For his part, Martin was guilty of one "crime," if you could call it that; he had consumed a few too many tequilas. He had no idea his follies could expose secret plans to build a huge Black Sands Resort and Hotel—right on the very beach where Nando and the turtles lived. He also had no idea his actions might be the catalyst for what could be the bloodiest moment of Esmeralda's long history—even worse than the infamous Taxi Slaughters.

When Gorde Tranquilleno heard the news was out about Martin's drunken follies with the turtles and Nando, he muttered, "Ijole! It was a secret. Can't anybody keep a secret any more!" He headed out to Martin's place, with vengeance in his heart and on the way heard a rumor about a resort being built on the black sand beach. "How can someone build a resort on land they don't even own?" Gorde yelled.

Adelante Cortez, the mayor of Esmeralda, cried in exasperation as he declared, "Why are the people on this Island always fighting progress and shooting themselves in the foot when it comes to improving their lives?"

Right now, Adelante Cortez desperately wanted all the attention to go somewhere else. If the media started snooping around, all kinds of things could be exposed. Being the mayor, and being the perpetrator or at least partner in all those things, namely the Black Sands Resort and Hotel, he just might end up in jail or worse. Not a pleasant prospect for a man who was fond of telling his friends, "I have life by the balls," and, in truth, on his little island, he did. But all that could change—now.

Stan Lovejoy, of Stan's Ice cream, just didn't trust the Mexican Government, or for that matter, any government and was adamantly opposed to any kind of development. "And that's why I live here," he told his customers as they devoured his delicious home made ice cream, "We don't have a real government here and we certainly don't need one. If that Pargo Cortez would keep his nose out of our business, we'd all be a lot better off."

Many of the islanders referred to Adelante Cortez as Pargo or Pargo Cortez—a Pargo being a local coral-eating fish with a hooked nose that was capable of killing the reef with its' voracious appetite. Adelante's nose did hook fiercely, very similar to a Pargo.

"That Pargo has been pecking away at our village for years," raged Stan, "and now this, this resort (which Stan immediately took on as a fact) is gonna be like a million Pargo attacking a reef all at once. It could destroy us!"

Both Vicente Fernandez and his archrival Paulo Gabernetti (who admittedly enjoyed sharing their monopoly of the island's taxi business) agreed the new resort, which they now also took as fact, would be great for their taxi companies cash flow. But in reality could be disastrous because, they both agreed for the first time in decades, they didn't want the island full of tourists and, God forbid, customers. They liked the way things were just fine, thank you.

And, of course, there were a few who actually favored the idea of the resort.

Alfredo Lopez Ramos, the mainland real-estate tycoon, wasn't "going to let a few fuckin' turtle eggs stop my project." If he could handle the governor, and the folks from Sedesol and Fonatour, he could take care of a few turtles and an old, frail Indian. After all, the Black Sands Resort was going to set him up for life. Alfredo knew just how he was going to solve the problem.

Whatever the case, it was a grand problem that no one wanted, especially the people of this sparsely populated island. How they were going to get out of this predicament was a mystery to all. The fact was the name Esmeralda was on the lips of people around the globe. The island where a lost breed of gigantic sea turtles had been discovered.

The island where an ancient man, said to be over one hundred and thirty years old, was still living a pre-Columbian lifestyle. The island, that in reality, never had been on the map, and had never wanted to be on the map, was making international headlines—all because of Martin.

Chapter 3

Of course, the island did have a long and illustrious history of "accidental" incidents that sometimes meant big trouble, sometimes little trouble, but always meant some kind of trouble, for somebody. Somehow, things always seemed to turn out okay, if not great for whoever had "spilled the beans" or "killed the bees." Call it fate. Call it luck. Blame it on the magic of the three turtles. On the whole, the people of Esmeralda were an extremely lucky bunch and now, they were really in the spotlight.

The tiny island had been in the spotlight before and survived. Like the time, back in the late 1950s, when Adolfo Lopez Mateos was elected President of Mexico. As a gracious and grand gesture, one that many presidents did as a sign of their power and as a "thank you" for votes, he gave money to Esmeralda to build their first city hall. Even though Esmeralda didn't have more than five hundred people living on the island at the time, it did have a beautiful and colorful location. The tropical flowers, white sand beaches, "grateful natives" all would make for good press. The public-relations people had felt they had picked the most scenic location in Mexico, and they were right.

So President Mateos gave the then newly elected mayor of Esmeralda, Adelante Cortez (who was a mere twenty years old and already famous for his hooked nose), a check for fourteen thousand pesos to build a city hall. And sure enough, the economy of Esmeralda boomed with full employment and the mayor and his cohorts talked about how the island was finally going to fight its way out of poverty.

Adelante Cortez thought it would be fitting to turn their city hall into a showcase of their incredible wealth of history. "After all," he said in one of the many town meetings that preceded the beginning of construction, "We're a unique village, with the three turtles and other items of interest, which really should be shared with the world."

Adelante loved the story of the three turtles and he wanted to use the sacred stones that had been found in the ruins on the other side of the island. It was a grand coming out, because these ruins, for centuries only seen by the wise men and shamans, would now be on public display, for all the citizens of Esmeralda to see. Adelante saw it as a grand opportunity to insure generations of political strength. His name would be next to the three turtles, a powerful symbol that had prevailed in their culture from the beginning of time, and his name would be forever remembered as the mayor who made it all happen.

Construction began and every now and again a Federal official would meet with Adelante Cortez, take a few pictures to show superiors back in Mexico City progress was indeed being made, and yes, they would be ready for the grand ribbon-cutting ceremony that was to be broadcast on national TV.

Of course, Adelante Cortez had failed to tell the Federal official of his grand surprise. He wanted to save it for the President. He could see it already. Pictures of himself and the President of the United States of Mexico, shaking hands right in front of the artifacts depicting the story of the three turtles. What more could a man, a politician, anyone for that matter, want out of life? And at the young age of twenty!

The precious stones were stored in a warehouse, next to the new city hall construction site, and when ordered by Adelante, they were installed into the exterior walls of the city hall building using a full six inches of cement. They would remain a part of Esmeralda's history for generations to come.

The fable of the three turtle's hieroglyphics told of the sighting of the three turtles by an old, wise Indian woman and her two children. The turtles had come to the village elders, asking for help because they were losing their breeding grounds. Legend had it that the village elders promised the turtles they would be protected and for this, the turtles had promised the villagers would be graced with long lives and eternal luck.

It was a story that every man, woman and child on the island knew by heart. And now, for the first time in the history of the island, the artifacts would be on view for the whole world to enjoy.

With a few helicopters flying over the island, patrol boats circling, and agents perched high on the buildings of little Isla Esmeralda, the President of Mexico arrived in full fanfare. The whole village was dressed in their Sunday best. Adelante Cortez stood next to the covered artifacts waiting for his moment of glory. Next to him stood his wife and new baby boy. He tried to keep a serene, official air about him, but he was so excited he could barely hold back his grin.

Time began to move rapidly for Adelante.

The car pulled up. The President came out. Flags waved. Adelante shook the president's hand. The President gave a speech. Cameras hummed. Photos flashed. The whole village was there. The whole country was there. Maybe the whole world, thought Adelante as he looked at the red lights on the TV cameras.

All smiles, the President turned to Adelante and motioned for him to unveil what by all rights should have been a brass placard with his name engraved on it.

Adelante moved over to the covered artifacts as slowly as his nervous, excited, body would allow him (he wanted all the photos possible taken of this historical moment). As he did, ten assistants moved to other areas of the newly completed building, ready to take off the straw-colored draping that was covering the mayor's grand surprise. In unison, the mayor and all of the assistants uncovered the huge, precious artifacts that were completely embedded in the walls. The crowd began a long, loud round of applause as they read the inscriptions and saw the story of the three turtles for the first time.

Above the three stones depicting the beginning of the three turtles' story, stood the inscription: Municipal de la Isla Esmeralda. 1958. Adelante Cortez—Mayor.

The President read this and looked for more. There was none. Then he looked at the artifacts. He had studied anthropology for a while at Harvard. Those looked like authentic, pre-Columbian. He turned to the smiling, beaming mayor and asked him if in fact they were real.

"Yes," Adelante beamed, and waving his hand in a grand fashion and almost yelling over the crowd's applause said, "We have a total of twelve precious artifacts we have carefully placed into our city hall. Aren't they just incredible?"

"Hump." Then a frown. A rich, dark red pulsed up from the president's neck to his cheek, then his forehead. A flurry of press agents and advisors rushed around in the background, with one coming right up to the President and reminding him that he was on national TV, that he should keep his composure and if he wanted to deal with the problem, here and now was exactly the wrong time to do it.

Still, the President couldn't hold himself back. The crowd, sensing something was about to happen quieted down just as the President turned to Adelante and angrily yelled, "They belong in a museum. In Mexico."

Adelante. Green mayor. Shaken dream. Speechless. Finally nodded and leaned into the microphone and said "No!"

The mayor, who in reality, was just mumbling no because he was seeing his future die right there before his eyes and the eyes of the village, the country, the world. One little mumble. He hadn't really meant it. But it was too late to take it back. The whole crowd has heard it. He saw the look of anger in the President's eyes. The crowd was reacting with applause and jeers. What had he done now?

It was just an accident, he wanted to yell. But he stood, stunned, in shock, watching his political life, his whole life, wash away like tiny specks of sand being carried out to sea by a stormy tide.

The President did a double take, and then moved away from the young kid, who looked like he was about to throw up. His advisors were right of course, he could take care of this battle tomorrow. Right now, he wanted to get off this godforsaken island and get back to his office.

Within five minutes the President was ushered off the island.

Unknowingly, Adelante had cemented his name into the hearts and souls of the citizens of Esmeralda. He had unwittingly accomplished his original goal. The crowd, to a person, immediately fell in love with their young mayor. They cheered for their new hero. The mayor who told the President of Mexico "no!" The mayor who stood up to the Feds and told them what to do with their big city museums. The artifacts belonged to the people of the island, and here they would stay. There would be songs written about Adelante. Mothers would tell their children about the day the mayor of Esmeralda had stood up to the Feds and told them, right to their face, "no!"

Adelante, not one to squander an opportunity, began to wave to the cheering crowds. Then he went to the microphone. "The artifacts are ours, and they will remain on Esmeralda, until the day I die." Adelante let the cheers wash over his drained body. Smiled. Waved. Stood tall and proud. Turned to his wife and whispered, "They love me."

And that was how the young mayor of Esmeralda, Adelante Cortez, fought and won the Artifact Wars against the Federal government so many, many years ago. Adelante should have been forever remembered as the hero-mayor who had stood up to the Mexican president for Esmeralda, except for one current bit of news—the Black Sands Resort.

Now the whole town could find out.

Not because Martin had told anyone. The only person Martin had told was Gorde the minute he had arrived back on the island. Gorde wouldn't tell a soul, at least while he was awake. When he was sleeping, that was another matter.

Anytime Gorde had something on his mind, he would toss and turn and talk and turn, all night long, repeating whatever was bothering him, over and over and over, until his wife, Vicki, would want to hit him over the head with a pillow. She sometimes did, waking up Gorde, who would startle, scream a few profanities and then fall right back to sleep, so fast, that Vicki didn't have a chance to fall asleep before him.

The night after Gorde spoke with Martin he had a lot on his mind. "What if the Feds find out about our secret…the turtles, the turtles," Gorde whispered in his sleep, a few times even yelling "no" at the top of his lungs. "They'll want to protect them, they'll end up dead." Over and over and over, "What about the turtles? What about Nando? How would he survive?"

And Vicki, who really didn't think she was "spilling beans," jokingly told a few of her friends about the discovery of Nando on the black sand beach, saying she had known about him all along, it was no big deal. But, the turtles, that could be a big deal, and Martin's survival, well, that was big news, which she proudly told her friends, saying to them, "Now don't tell anyone else, okay. But I heard they might even be building a resort and…"

Vicki's friends told their friends, saying not to tell anyone, and so on and so on, until the whole village knew about Martin's adventure with Nando and the turtles. This was pretty big news in Esmeralda. But so far, the people of Esmeralda didn't fully believe the news about the Black Sands Resort, which, if they believed was true, would have been more than big news; it would have been a revolution.

Chapter 4

It's a Mexican Peyton Place. If you sneeze, the guy lying in a hammock three miles down the beach says, "salud." Gorde Tranquilleno

Life is a soap opera. It was the one underlying fact Gorde absolutely knew about life. "Life is a soap opera," Gorde mused, "because everyone wants to know the truth, everyone wants to feel important, everyone, to a person, really can't keep a secret." He was angry. It was the day after he had told Martin to keep his mouth shut and he was already hearing about the turtles through the grapevine. The Gringo had spilled his guts to someone.

Gorde pulled up to Martin's compound and then busted through the huge front door with wild messy hair, tequila and sangrita on his breath (as well as his shirt). And, even though his body was trying to move slowly and gracefully, the amount of alcohol in his veins, along with a fair amount of adrenaline, was causing him to sway and list like a buoy lost in the high seas. Gorde made a few awkward pirouettes, scouting for possible listeners, saw Martin out on the verandah overlooking what was still the world's prettiest beach, and rushed over to him. All two hundred fifty-eight pounds of Gorde shook like an overstuffed washing machine. He hovered over Martin for a moment, literally blocking out the sun, intent on getting to the bottom of this, and then picked him up high in the air.

"My friend," Gorde slurred, in an angry yet conciliatory tone, "We have a saying on this island, "I won't spill the beans, if you keep refrying them."

Martin, high in the air, all six foot four inches at least four feet off the ground, looked down at Gorde in shock. He didn't quite know what to say. What did the big man want?

Gorde, thinking Martin didn't understand him, said, "It means, a secret is a secret...I thought we had agreed that you were not going to tell anyone about the turtles."

"I didn't," Martin said, while his shirt started to rip. And then, suddenly, he was back on the ground—his shirt completely ripped off his back. But Gorde didn't even flinch. In fact, he still looked up at the empty shirt.

"The town is talking...the word is out. It will create problems," Gorde said.

Even though he was drunk and normally a jovial kind of guy, right now he was a serious little buoy floating on the seas of concern. He looked again, realizing that Martin was now standing on the terrace.

"The only person I told was you," Martin pleaded. "I swear, just you."

"Me? Only me?"

"Are you sure you didn't tell anybody?" Martin joked.

Gorde's eyes rolled back in his head. He swayed left, then right, then gently rolled backwards until his huge butt touched the ground, and with contact, he sat and thought for a good long while.

"Aaaaay Carumba! I don't remember telling anyone." Gorde yelled, then, suddenly mellow, "Do you want some tequila and sangrita. It's a good batch today."

The pain in his eyes revealed a truth, if not the truth of the matter. He had told someone about Martin's beach escapades. Martin walked Gorde back to his place to mix a drink when suddenly Gorde figured out how the word had gotten out. He grabbed his head, then his chest like he was having a heart attack and yelled in a high pitched voice, "Aaaaay Carumba, Vicki. The whole town will know."

Martin, after he realized Gorde wasn't dying on his steps, soon learned that Gorde had probably mumbled his secret in his sleep. After Gorde had explained what he thought had happened Martin tried to comfort him.

"It's okay. It's not the end of the world," Martin said, reassuringly.

"Oh my friend, if you only knew," Gorde sputtered, turned around a few times then sat down on his tail again and passed out.

Chapter 5

Adelante Cortez finished off his morning set of singles tennis with a powerful overhead smash. Game, set, match. "Thank goodness," he whispered to himself. It was starting to get hot and he knew if it went another game or two it was anybody's set. The mayor didn't like to lose, and rarely did.

Adelante looked out over the horizon and saw his huge flock of pigeons circling his hillside estate not more than a few miles away. He had been raising pigeons for over twenty years now. What started out as a great form of entertainment soon turned into a passion. Adelante loved his pigeons and they returned the favor by providing him with a delicate meat for his table. He saw the lead pigeon take a tumble, fall toward the earth and then recover, as if nothing had happened. He was always amazed how no matter what, the flock always followed the lead bird back to the cage. Even if a few of the birds were missing in the morning, they always came back sooner or later. His birds astonished him with their loyalty. All you had to do was give them a little food and water, and they were happy. "A lot like the villagers," he thought as he took a long swig of water.

In fine shape for a man who just turned sixty, he was a master of control in the game of tennis, and in the game of life. He always started his tennis matches at dawn. He knew if he let the heat of the day wear him down he would run out of gas and possibly lose. So three times a week, around six-thirty in the morning, Adelante met his opponent and tried to wrap things up by nine.

This morning's victim was Ramon Ramiriz, the Chief of Police. Fifteen years younger than Adelante, Ramon was a formidable player. Adelante used his top-spin lob, his consistent forehand and his backhand slice to slowly wear down the Chief of Police, and in the end, it was a too close 6-4, 4-6, 7-5. One of Adelante's longest matches he'd had in many a year.

Adelante wiped the sweat off his forehead, shook hands with Ramon and thanked him for the game. Both men packed up their equipment in the quickly warming morning sun.

"Have you heard about the survivor?" the Chief of Police said, breaking their silence.

"No. What survivor?"

"A man survived a night on the black sands beach."

"Go on," Adelante said.

Ramon Ramiriz gave a detailed version of Martin's turtle adventure. He told of a man who came back from the forbidden beach, with only a sunburn. He told of the awe it had stirred up in the village. He ended his story with a brief description of an absurd rumor that "the survivor," as they had started to call Martin, had seen a masked Indian and turtle eggs on the beach.

"Better yet," the chief laughed, "some people say there will be a resort built on this same beach. Can you image that? Huh."

Adelante, a bit startled, steadied himself quickly and looked at the Chief of Police for the first time and smiled, "How ridiculous, turtles on our island. Resorts. What some people will do to create a good story."

And then he dropped the subject, like a coconut falling from a huge tree. If it was true, it could be trouble, maybe even ruin him, because Adelante, in his old age, wanting to retire in a comfortable Acapulco high-rise, had stuck out his neck…far. He had, for the first time in his life of politics, done something, that if revealed, could get him kicked out of office or worse. He had said yes to Alfredo Lopez Ramos, the developer who had approached him a year earlier about purchasing land on the island.

At first, Adelante had told him land couldn't really be sold on the island, because since the revolution and Zapata the whole island was considered the people's island. If you live on a piece of land, it was considered yours, until you moved. But you didn't own it, you couldn't really sell it.

"I'm sure we can arrange something," Alfredo Lopez Ramos had urged Adelante. And then, Alfredo made his usual offer, thinking that this small town mayor would probably say no.

"Why don't we go to Acapulco and discuss the matter further," Alfredo had said, "and maybe I can get some friends to join us."

"Acapulco…sure," Adelante had said. Adelante had been to Acapulco once and loved it. It was his dream to go back there and retire.

By the end of the three day weekend they had cooked up a way for Adelante to not only own most of the island, but a way for him to actually sell the black sand beach area to Alfredo for a fine profit.

"It works like this," Alfredo had told Adelante. "You post signs all along the island. They have to be up for a week or two. But you can make them real complicated, fine print, legalese, so nobody really reads them. They state that if you are living on the island, you can legally register your property with the Land Bureau of Esmeralda. We've been doing this all over Mexico. It allows us to control the land. If we want some property, we just raise the taxes so the people can't pay and we go in and take it. Legally."

"Legally," Adelante had questioned. "With laws like that, who needs enemies?"

"Then, they have one day to come in, register their property, paying a small fee," Alfredo said, rubbing the gold chain around his neck, leaning in to Adelante and in a whisper, finishing with, "If they don't come in, in ten days it goes to the Land Bureau. But here's the catch. After ten days, you can register the property in your name, if you pay a large fee. Make it a fee that most people on the island can't afford. So you don't have others competing with you."

"I don't think it will work. The people on my island won't register for anything. They still haven't gotten used to using money," Adelante said.

"Fine. Even better. You will probably own the whole island then. I only want a little piece. The rest can be yours. And when the resort goes in, land prices will skyrocket my friend. You'll be a millionaire. You'll be able to buy your own highrise in Acapulco!"

Adelante had followed the developer's plan to a tee. He had posted the signs and had the day of registration on a Sunday, knowing that nobody on the island would show up on a Sunday. A few people did arrive, but on a whole, Adelante Cortez was the proud owner of the Island of Esmeralda. At least on paper.

That is why when he heard about the turtle sighting on his beach, his blood pressure went up. He had read about what had happened at other resorts when rare animals had been discovered. Projects had been stopped. Millions lost. Even worse, if the islander's found out about Adelante's involvement in the project, he wouldn't even wait to be voted out of office, because if they truly found out what he had been up to, he was a dead man, plain and simple.

Chapter 6

Four men were sitting around the table in a secret conference room nestled in a high rise in Mexico City. Rafael Cuevas Delgado, the state governor of the area who thought he had jurisdiction over Esmeralda, was a tall, lanky man who dressed impeccably and rarely let anything get by him. He was concerned over the rumor of turtles being found on the beach in Esmeralda. Not just any kind of turtles, but leatherback turtles, perhaps a rare breed thought to be extinct. If it were true, they'd have to find another suitable site for the resort; which was not likely, since there weren't many islands off the coast and the mainland was already way too congested. The Governor knew, with the current public opinion on environmental issues, that he had to play this one very safely. He was not going to stick his neck out and get it cut off, no way. Still, he needed the money, the tax base, to get a few of his pet projects completed.

Also in the room was Roberto Cristanto of the Mexican Tourist conglomerate Fonatour, along with his partner in crime, Javiar Garcia Sanchez from Social Development Secretary (Sedesol), and the developer on the Esmeralda project, Alfredo Lopez Ramos, who had originally found out about the problem. He had worked with Roberto and Javiar on numerous other projects, including turning the five bays of Hualtulco into a modern day Alcapulco.

Alfredo sat nervously jingling his thick gold chain on his wrist. The chain matched the one on his neck, that matched the one he had dangling from his new Cadillac in the parking lot. He was still kicking himself for not annexing Esmeralda last year when they had first come up with the plan to build a resort on the island. But no, Roberto and Javiar said it wouldn't be a problem. Don't worry, they had assured him, it will all come with time. Now he was hearing differently. And he didn't like what he heard.

As the governor got up and paced the room, looking out the window, the three men eyed each other, knowing Rafael Cuevas Delgado as they did, his body language was scaring the daylights out of them. Pacing. Stiff. Worried. This was going to be a tough one for the three of them. The Governor, who had the power to kill their project, wasn't one to move without all the information laid out in a clear-cut fashion.

"Tell me what you know," the Governor asked the room in a concerned voice. Again, the three men looked at each other, who was going to start? They hadn't had a chance to talk in advance because of the urgency of the meeting. They had all been called in separately, on short notice.

Finally, Alfredo the developer, who didn't know much about the facts but knew if he didn't get talking he was going to loose a bundle, started with: "We know that so far there hasn't been a documented sighting of a leatherback on the island. Everything is heresay."

When the Governor didn't react, didn't even look up, Alfredo began to talk a little faster, more urgently, hoping to convince him that everything really was okay. After a few more minutes, with Alfredo repeating over and over that there really hadn't been a documented sighting, the room, completely still except for the governor's pacing and the other people's hearts racing, began to feel a little claustrophobic to the three men.

The undersecretary of Social Development, Javiar Garcia Sanchez, realizing the Governor was reacting in a negative way to Alfredo, calmly cut Alfredo off with: "I really don't think this is the issue. Whether there really was an actual sighting or not. If we know about this rumor, the whole island does too. Besides, there are some options we can pursue with or without the turtles."

"I still don't believe there are turtles," Alfredo nervously piped in, giving Javiar a look of, whose side are you on anyway?

The Governor turned, looked Javiar in the eyes and calmly asked, "what do you suggest Javiar?"

"Well, for one" Javiar slowly and carefully said, "we could build a turtle museum on the site, make it a part of the complex. If we do have turtles that is."

"Humm. Interesting idea. I like that," the Governor said as he sat back down, relaxing a little.

Javiar took the floor for a while, now that the Governor was sitting, and painted the picture of a turtle museum as part of the massive hotel complex. It was a nice image, one that would keep the Governor off our back, thought Javiar, until we take care of the problem.

And so, after five more minutes of Javiar calmly reviewing the current facts he knew, which wasn't much, and the hotel complex now saved, for the time being, the meeting was called to an end by the Governor getting up and saying, "Thank you gentlemen, it seems we have ironed out a good solution that will keep all parties happy. Proceed, but please keep me posted."

With that, Alfredo, Javiar and the ever-silent representative of Fonatur, Roberto Crisanto, were excused and walked out the hallway and into the elevator. "Jesus Roberto," Alfredo accused, "why didn't YOU say anything."

"I hate to say it guys, but we're in trouble," Roberto said. "Haven't you looked at the plans? We can't build a museum on the site. We really don't even have enough workable ground as it is. Besides, we can't use the beach if it has turtles on it. The Feds will close us down before we even get started. They'll go above Delgado's head and cancel the whole project." He turned to Alfredo and whined, "Remember what happened in Monterey three years ago."

Alfredo didn't like the sound of this, and nearly shaking again, in a quavery voice, with spit flying said, "We can take care of those turtles. Don't you worry about those little suckers. I'm not letting a few fuckin' turtles stop this project, do you two hear me, I'm not, I'm not."

Both Roberto and Javiar, in their heart of hearts, truly disliked Alfredo. They didn't like his cocaine habit, they didn't like his fast-talking, but he was, they had to admit, one of the best developers in the country. He got things done. He didn't mind getting his hands dirty if he had too, and it looked like, in this instance, he was going to get his hands very, very dirty.

"Just let me take care of it," Alfredo urged, "there won't be another word about turtles within fifty miles of Esmeralda." Roberto and Javiar silently nodded their heads, with Javiar saying in the end, as they left the elevator and went their separate ways, "We'll give you a week."

Chapter 7

In the cover of night three poachers silently drove their fishing boat toward the small island one hundred and fifty miles south of their harbor. They had been paid handsomely for a chore that some Mexican men these days would probably do for free, if they had the opportunity. As the turtles began to disappear from the beaches, getting and eating turtle eggs was becoming an extremely difficult proposition. All the beaches that still had turtles coming onto the shore to lay their eggs were protected by law. Theoretically, the turtles were protected. It was illegal to hunt them, eat their eggs, drink their blood or in anyway disturb their nest. In reality, things were a little different.

The demand for turtle eggs had seemingly increased when they had become illegal. Eating turtle eggs was a passion, a true sign of virility. Many men believed it actually helped you to become more virile. So the market for these eggs, even though they were now illegal, was huge. In Mexico City, one could make a very good living supplying the high-end bars with eggs, if you could find them.

Alfredo had given them special instructions to get every single egg. It would be like the old days for these veteran poachers, the days when you could just stroll onto a beach late at night and take your pick of the crop. These days the poachers mostly worked the water. Normally "trolling for fish" as their cover, then jumping over the side of the boat, grabbing the unsuspecting turtle, quickly cutting out the eggs and discarding the rest. It was a waste of good meat and shell, but the poachers couldn't take the chance of getting caught with a turtle in their boat. If the Federales, whom they rarely saw, did pursue them, they could always claim they were just trolling and drop their eggs, (which were always attached to a weight just for this purpose) over the side of the boat and they were evidence free.

They thought the island, which they had heard of and never visited, probably didn't have many eggs. They had never heard of eggs on Esmeralda, and they had been poaching for over twenty years. It seemed like a pretty easy assignment, even though it needed to be completed within three days.

They entered the bay with the black sand beach, dropped anchor, and swam with flashlights in hand, to the hard packed sand. The huge Emerald Bellys were literally walking right past them. Even the poachers didn't notice the difference between the Emerald Belly and a standard Leatherback. Underneath, on their belly, right in the middle, was a small emerald dot, about the size of a dime, or a bee.

The poachers found a few eggs and were amazed at the size and quality of their find. They had never seen eggs so big or so tasty. So they ate, until their stomachs were full, and without even leaving the hard sand, started to fill up the huge white coffee-bean bags they brought, just in case a miracle such as this may happen.

They joked about it being like the old days, rode on the backs of a few turtles like they were riding bucking broncos and yelled at the top of their lungs. With dollar signs in their eyes, eggs in their stomachs and images of their customers paying twice, maybe three times as much as normal, the three men dug into a few nests close to the surf line. They found huge caches of eggs, larger than anything they had seen in their twenty years of working the beaches. They were astounded at the quality and the abundance of the eggs. They couldn't take all of them—not only because there were too many, but also because, this quality of egg was a gold mine for them. Greed dictated they only take three bags full, leaving the rest for next year, and the year after, and the year after.

"We haven't even worked the soft sand," one of them said, as he carried one of the bags to the boat, "there must be thousands of eggs sitting there for the taking."

They all agreed if the word got out, the value of the eggs would drop and they'd probably be all gone in one year anyway. It would be their little secret, their little gold mine.

Meanwhile, as the men left the beach with Three bags full of eggs, Nando, who had been high above in the mountains sweating in his temescal (he did this one night a month or when he needed to think about something important), returned to his home and was startled to feel that some eggs had been taken from his beach. He could also feel that it was over, for now. But he would have to be prepared for war. The war that he had been having premonitions about, was close at hand.

Three days later, when the poachers reported back to Alfredo, they told him they had in fact, carted away three huge bags of turtle eggs, and that yes, they had taken every egg on the beach. So, with this information in hand, Alfredo called up his compadres and set up a meeting. He informed them that the beach did in fact have "a few eggs" that were nothing to be concerned about because, in fact, they were no longer on the beach. With this announcement, he brandished six chicken-sized eggs, hoping to celebrate their victory with a taste of this rare catch. Both Roberto and Javiar declined, but thanked Alfredo for taking care of business and suggested that another meeting with the Governor were in order.

Chapter 8

En Casa del Herrerro Asadon de palo.
In the house of ironworkers are tools of wood.

After all of the excitement of the first week, Martin began to settle in to his place. He soon found he didn't have hot water hooked up to his sink, and he sometimes didn't get it in the shower, where it was plumbed, and every once in a while, he would run out of water completely. Martin learned, soon enough, that he was living UPTOWN, and that the rest of the village used outhouses and washed in the river. So, he couldn't complain, in fact, he thought for a while that it might even be a better solution to just give in to the water problem and do like the natives. But somehow, when he was at the depths of his water woes, his landlord Sergio would always come around and tell him everything was all right, not to worry and the water would flow.

Martin's place was just outside of the town of Esmeralda, one of eight homes clustered together overlooking the most beautiful beach in the world (white sand, palm trees, a crescent shaped bay about one hundred and fifty yards across that was protected from the high surf and the winds). When entering his home one got the feeling that they were looking out a huge porthole. The building was about fifteen feet wide and one hundred and twenty feet long, the width determined by the land since it was built into a cliff.

Four fifths of the ocean side was covered with windows or screens, looking out on two small balconies that could be accessed via a beautifully decorated sliding wooden door. On each balcony two chairs and a small table awaited visitors. The floors of the balcony, in fact the whole house, were comprised of used brick sprinkled with blue, green and yellow bird shaped tiles called Azulejos.

A person could walk into this home and forget about the outside world. They could, in fact, forget about everything except the beautiful sound of the crashing surf, the soft, silky message of the daily ocean breeze, the incredible sunsets of this tropical paradise—all viewed through a few palm fronds from the higher trees; definitely off the map.

In fact, the Island of Esmeralda itself was literally, off the map: it had never officially been considered a part of Mexico. The island had had no armed forces, no sales tax, no income tax, no tax period.

The post-office was a huge P.O. box on the mainland that was picked clean once a week by a local fisherman. The government had just about always been Adelante Cortez—a kind of one-man unofficial un-dictatorial dictator.

Yup, if one dreamed of dropping out and finding "paradise" Esmeralda was a prime choice. An island off the map because, frankly, nobody knew what to do with this little strip of coral and mud and beehives. If you wanted to get lost and not found, this was definitely the place.

The beach was accessed by a long flight of stairs. These were not ordinary stairs, as each step had been hand crafted. At the top, the stairs were about ten feet wide and as they went down, they got narrower and narrower. There were three hundred and twenty-four steps in all. Every one went straight up, or down, and they all were a different size, angle and camber.

It was as if the person who had built them didn't realize what he or she was in for, and when they got about ten stairs down, they decided to make an adjustment. Another twenty, we better make these suckers a little narrower. This is a lot of work. Thirty more down, I think we should just put slabs of cement, forget all the pretty adornments. Either side of the stairs was usually a ten-foot drop, sometimes, a drop to death. The key was not to look down, around, anywhere except to the next step.

Martin remembered how the first two days in paradise he had thought he was coming down with some sort of strange tropical disease.

Exhausted at night from all his adventure on the black sand beach, he had started to go up and down the stairs daily and on the third night his calves cramped and ached. At first, he thought it was from the beach ordeal and paddling, but then, on the third day, the day he ended up taking the stairs twice, the second time up he counted the stairs.

The "Mexican Stair Step" method to rock hard legs in one month can't fail," he whispered. "My lungs and heart, on the other hand, could."

When he asked Sergio about the stairs he was told each year, when the rains came, a different part of the stairs would get washed out. It was obvious to Martin that some years Sergio felt more industrious than others. One part of the stairs, he noticed, was simply piled up rocks made to look like stairs. Another part, beautifully hand made steps with individual Mexican designs artfully carved into each step. But whether it was an industrious year or just a pile of rocks, the thing that made them so hard to climb was the various heights and the unadulterated steepness of each and every step.

The stairs were designed for giants. To be able to comfortably ascend each step you'd need to be twenty feet tall. This had caused some problems over the years.

For instance, about five years ago an older couple, Angel and Rosaria Hernandez, were walking up the stairs, when they slipped on some sand and went over the edge. Angel, in his late sixties, and his beautiful wife, herself sixty-three (although she told anyone who asked forty-five) both were knocked out instantaneously.

When they didn't come home that night their children (Rosarita, Angelito, Humberto, Layi and Chuco) were worried sick. They called the police, thinking maybe there was some kind of foul play. They sent out search parties in the night looking for their beloved parents. They even went so far as to ask the three turtles for help. But nothing worked. Come morning the whole town was hoping for the best, but fearing the worst.

The whole town, that is, except Angel and Rosaria. When they had come to, in the middle of the night, they were both lying on soft sand, a warm body and, of course, in total darkness. Angel didn't know if he was in heaven or hell, all he did know was that his wife was next to him—warm, soft and particularly inviting.

For her part, Rosaria was groggy and felt about how she had felt when she was sixteen and had her first drink. She was giggling, partly cause she was glad to be alive and mostly because her man, all sixty-eight years of him, was rubbing up against her body with the biggest erection he'd had in twenty years. They made love. Fell asleep. Woke up. Made love again. Then, as the morning sun came up over the horizon, they watched the ballet-like movement of the orange and black butterflies of Esmeralda float in the pale, pink air of the sunrise. Slowly they dusted off their bruised yet satisfied bodies, and limped up the rest of the stairs.

When they came through the gate and sauntered into the compound, just about the time the morning search party was completely formed and ready for the next hunt, they were met with wide-eyed wonder. Angel still had his erection. Rosaria was still giggling under her breath.

"Are you two okay. What happened?" Angelito asked.

"We fell off the stairs," Angel grinned, "into another time. A good time."

Then Angel proceeded to tell all fifteen or so of the people who were on the terrace about his travels to another world. How he and Rosaria had been swept away into this world, where everything was soft, warm and loving.

The group stood in wonder. Some grinned, noticing Angel's erection. Others smiled, realizing that Rosaria couldn't stop giggling. A few of them were a bit angry; they had been up all night searching for these two, and obviously, they had been out partying, having a great time. But to a person, they were all very relieved that Angel and Rosaria were okay.

And to a person, they believed it was the three turtles that had watched over their parents, their friends, their Esmeraldians. A silent prayer of thanks went out to the turtles.

Now, five years later, Martin was on his way down to the beach for a swim. He needed to relax a bit and, he promised himself, no paddling out into the bay and falling asleep. To get there, he opened the very same gate that Angel and Rosaria had passed through years ago when they returned from their adventure.

When Martin passed through the gate his knit backpack broke and all his beach apparel, as well as his Spanish/English dictionary, notebook and sunglasses went falling to the ground. They landed just inside the gate, where a twenty by forty-foot platform formed the entrance to the Mexican Stair Step routine.

Martin slowly picked up his belongings and when he leaned over for his last item he looked up and saw a huge snake curled up on the first step. He froze. Then slowly started to back up. The snake, about five feet long, was brown and beige with a distinct diamond shape head. Martin checked out the head. He'd always been told that diamond-shaped heads were dangerous. But he didn't know for sure and he wasn't about to find out either. He slowly backed up to the gate, fiddled with the lock, trying not to make any noise. I don't want to give him any excuse for striking, Martin thought.

When he backed inside the gate he found Sergio and Gloria relaxing on the terrace. Martin, a bit whiter than normal, a bit shaken, proclaimed, "There is a snake out there. And, it's big."

"No problem," Sergio confidently said, "I'll take care of it."

He went off to his casita and came back with a long spear-like piece of metal that had a piece of rubber looped into a circle. "I'll just catch him, take him off the trail. It'll be okay. Come on."

Martin paused, then decided, "why not?" Sergio knows what he's doing. Sergio opened the gate, took one look at the snake and exclaimed, "Ijole. It's a giant. I'll be right back," and ran back to his house.

Martin, thinking that Sergio was going to get his camera, ran to his place, grabbed his camera (he didn't want to miss a photo opportunity) and came back onto the platform, only to find Sergio aiming his rifle at the snake. Martin wanted to tell Sergio to stop. He didn't want the snake killed. The snake hadn't done anything to him. But Sergio shot, two times, hitting his target with both bullets. On the second shot Martin lowered his camera and took a picture. Sergio walked up to the snake, moved it a few times with his rifle and when it was apparent that the snake was dead, he picked it up with his rifle and draping it over the barrel, held it up to Martin.

"Take a photo. This is the biggest Atuzi I have ever seen," Sergio said.

"Did you have to kill it?" Martin asked.

"Martin. One bite from an Atuzi and you are dead within five minutes. I had to kill it."

With this new information, and with his hands shaking uncontrollably, Martin lowered his camera and took a photo of Sergio, who smiled like a great white elephant hunter with his kill. The Atuzi stretched out a full five feet in length.

"You are lucky to be alive, my friend," Sergio smiled, "usually these snakes strike at anything within twenty feet of their perimeter and they can jump out a full fifty feet, no problem. I think maybe the three turtles have adopted you."

Maybe it was this new bit of information, maybe it was the heat, or maybe it was that Martin had just had a long, long week, with the black sand beach incident. Whatever the case, with this statement Martin promptly fainted, falling slowly to the ground like one of Stan's ice cream cones melting in the heat of the tropical sun.

Chapter 9

"Let the bees do the work."
An Esmeraldian folk saying

In reality, some kind of drama was always occurring on Esmeralda, usually at a much smaller scale though. For instance, over the years three different states from the mainland decided they liked the idea of taxing the islanders for their land. So, at various times, they tried to tax the populace of Esmeralda, and, each time, after months, sometimes years of struggles, the tax collectors left frustrated. They would report back to the state that "the people don't have any money, so how can we tax them?"

One year, with a new governor in power, the plan was to inject the economy of Esmeralda with some hard cash, so it would be theirs for the taxing. So, at great expense to the taxpayers of Mexico, the governor commissioned some experts to formulate a plan to guide the island toward a cash-based economy.

The only plan the commission could realistically propose was to increase the honey production. A huge document, over fifty pages, was compiled with graphs and charts, showing the possibilities of exporting Esmeralda's rare wild honey to the world.

It was true that the bees accomplished the only real work done on the island. The saying "Let the bees do the work," was a favorite one of Esmeraldians, and work they did. Millions of bees called the island of Esmeralda their home. For generations nearly all the people of Hermana "worked" as bee tenders. Which, on the island, wasn't a very taxing proposition. Usually it entailed collecting the specially made honey every now and again. The honey was made from rare and beautiful tropical flowers that could only be found on the island. This made Esmeralda's honey unique and, the villagers believed, very powerful.

Adelante, proud mayor of Esmeralda, was easily sold on the idea of more and he pushed hard to implement it. However, the people who lived in Hermana, a small village on the other side of the island, who were the main bee keepers and had been practicing their art for generations, weren't happy with the idea of "experts" coming in to change their traditional methods of production. Sure, the traditional methods were very time consuming and when it came to mass production, very inefficient. But, it was the way they did things in Hermana. They had worked with the bees for generations and had a good partnership.

So, when government experts came in and pushed their new ways of production, the people resisted. Not overtly, because the people of Hermana were a very quiet, polite people who always greeted their guests with open arms, inviting them into their homes.

The mainland bee experts stayed at a few homes in the village (there were no hotels, after all) and tried to work their magic with one test location. They built hives, cleared away the land, and spent a lot of time and money working the bees into a fury. Unfortunately, the bee population, not as polite and friendly as the local people, didn't cooperate with the workers. In fact, when one of the experts, Hernando Balesco, tried to collect his first batch of test honey, he was stung so many times he had to be shipped off to the mainland for medical attention.

After the first successful test, which showed a double in production, the village elders, concerned that the techniques the "experts" were using could lead to problems, needed to air out their concerns. So, over a formal (for Hermana) dinner, they discussed their concerns, the main one being that at this rate of production the bees were bound to get tired and if they did tire out, they would stop working. How could they hold up over the years at that rate?

The experts assured the elders all would be well. Still, the villagers said, maybe they could go back and ask the government for some kind of insurance. The experts agreed because they knew the elders did have a point. Their production techniques were designed to get the very most honey at a time, not worrying about the long term effects on the bees.

In record time, only a month, the experts reappeared with a promise from the Mexican Government that if the bees failed the village would be generously compensated. The elders looked over the promise, asked Adelante for advice, and, when everything looked safe, signed away their bees.

Of course all went as planned the first two years. But in the third year, the bees, exhausted and needing a rest, retreated to the high mountains of Esmeralda, refusing to produce honey of any consequence. So the elders contacted the experts, and when they came out to check the hives, they had to admit, production wasn't only down, it was dead. The hives had failed and the village would have to be compensated. But the state didn't quite see it that way, and they failed to pay. The consequences were dire. Many of the villagers, now without honey to barter, had to move to Esmeralda.

The population of Hermana went from one hundred and twenty to forty within a year. The hives were closed down and the elders, angry not only at the mainland, but Adelante as well, marched on city hall.

"I am not the villain," Adelante told the angry machete-welding crowd, "the government of the mainland guaranteed the money. I will help you get it." And he tried, he truly did, but it was hard to get money from a government that officially didn't recognize you. And when the word of the bee failure got out, nobody wanted to touch Esmeralda.

So, the money never came, but a few years later, with the help of a little coaxing from the remaining people in Hermana, the bees did return. A few of the people who had fled the village returned, but many, being younger and now settled with kids and friends in Esmeralda, stayed in their new homes and worked the bees from a distance.

So, with the bees back, the island of Esmeralda was once again a buzzing, productive land, with a special honey that was said to have magical powers.

Chapter 10

"Mista, you're nothing but a Pendejo!"
Magda

Special honey had not always played a big role in the lives of Esmeraldian's. But the story of how it had come about was a major part of the local folklore. Many years ago, when Gorde Tranquilleno was just a young pike, (before his mother Magda had started throwing limes at passerby) Magda used to go up into the hills for hours on end to gather wood. She always took her favorite burro named Bromista.

These days Bromista wasn't much to look at that was for sure. He was considered undersized in height, a little fat around the belly and when he moved around on crooked-spindly legs, every step looked like it was his last. His feet, which admittedly could use a lot of work, hit the dirt trails with a sullen clop and froze, as if he was stuck in cement, and then, after a long pause, pulled out before he was stuck for eternity.

His gait, if you could call it that, was more Tin Man than burro, because while his feet froze, the rest of his body continued on down the line until the sheer power of velocity and gravity forced each foot to lift off the ground. And when that happened, he took another step, which started the whole process over again.

With tiny little gray ears, pink on the inside, and red saggy eyes that looked like they hadn't slept in a lifetime, Bromista's head wiggled like one of those toy dogs in the back-seat of a car. Needless to say, he wasn't going to win any beauty contests (not that they had any for the burros on the island).

But Bromista wasn't always this beat up and over the hill.

Many, many years ago, when Bromista was a young buck and carried five times his weight in fire wood on a daily basis (no wonder his legs were shot), he was in the high mountains when the incident happened. Magdelena had stacked a huge load of wood on him in preparation for a three turtles fiesta about to take place. Then, after she tied him off, she went back into the woods and didn't return.

At first Bromista thought she was after more wood, but within ten minutes he knew something was wrong. She had never left him standing with a full load of wood before, not this long. She had always, thankfully, headed directly home. They had been doing this routine for over ten years. They had become pretty close over the years. Best friends. Bromista brayed to Magda and she talked to him…a lot. About the problems in the village, local gossip, anything that Magda needed to get off her chest, without worrying that word would get back to town.

Now Bromista let out a loud hee-haw for Magda. No response. He looked to his left, then his right, and finally, deciding that he needed to get off the dirt trail and do some investigating, tried to buck off his wood load. One kick and down tumbled a full days worth of work, making the kind of noise Bromista knew would wake the dead, and hopefully he thought, the living.

Right now, he wanted nothing more than to have Magda come running out of the woods, yelling at him "Mista, You're nothing but a Pendejo!"

He waited, nearly getting down on four knees and praying for her to come out and yell at him. Silence.

Magda, on the other hand, was not, at the moment very silent. Just minutes before, for the first time in her life, she had felt a strange feeling well up inside her chest, a feeling that time was running out, that if she didn't get back to the village with her load of wood, that something terrible would happen to her. She couldn't pin point exactly what this would be if she didn't move fast, but it would be horrific—she knew that.

She had never experienced this feeling. She wondered what it was called, if there was a name for it, and wished, oh wished, to the almighty Tre Turtles, that it would go away.

Still, she moved a little quicker than usual and worried about time for the first time in her life. In short, she was in a rush. She had in fact come running in for one more load of wood. "Just one more quick load," she had whispered to herself as she entered the woods. But, as she rushed to pick up her load, she smashed into a palm tree, cursed out loud, bent over to pick up the dropped wood and was hit square on the head by a coconut.

It was her first, and maybe her last bit of bad luck in her life. She tumbled backwards, then forwards, dropping the wood all over the ground as she staggered in circles.

But Magda was a fighter, and she thought that someone had actually hit her over the head with something, so she fought the urge to fall. She fought and fought and fought, circling around like a dazed boxer who had gone one too many rounds. And as she staggered, she moved closer and closer to the sandy edge of the giant cliffs, which had been there from the beginning of time, and would be there when Magda and all the other living things on this island were long gone. And she fell. It wasn't a free fall but more of a tumble, as she continued to fight the urge to go down. End over end, with her head plopping against the soft sides of the top part of the cliff, then, luckily she changed into a side roll, safely rolling down the hard, steep edges of the cliff.

About half way down, again her luck returned. Instead of falling to her death, the shrubs and trees caught her. Hung up on a medium sized palm tree and a young mango tree, Magda lay semi-unconscious, cursing at the palm trees, at life itself. She was in a predicament.

Why would someone want to hurt her? What was that feeling she had had just before the attackers came after her? Back at the top of the cliff, about only two hundred yards away, but just outside of hearing distance, Mista could no longer wait. He walked off in the direction he had seen Magda enter the woods. Within two minutes, after passing her stacks of wood dispersed in a strange circular pattern, he followed her footsteps to the edge of the cliff. Looking over the cliff, he saw his friend hanging onto her life by the strength of her shirt.

Bromista brayed to her. She looked up, in a daze. Had it been Bromista who attacked her? Impossible. He must have warded off the attackers. "*Mista ayudame*. Help me."

Bromista pranced back and forth at the top of the cliff. It was now dark but a full moon helped to illuminate Magda. Bromista, himself feeling an urgency he'd never felt before, couldn't make up his mind: Should I go back to the village for help, or try to save her. He didn't want to let her out of his sight. It seemed like any minute she could fall to her death. He knew he had to act, and act fast.

What happened next will live on in the history of the islands journals, for whether he flew, slid, walked or ran, somehow, Bromista made his way down to where the woozy Magda hung on for dear life. He snapped her up like a vulture grabbing a dead rabbit and magically flew, ran, to within ten feet of the top of the cliff. There he promptly landed, stumbled and with one final push from his nose, Magda was on safe ground, hanging on for dear life to Bromista's ears.

But…now, there was one small problem. Bromista had somehow suddenly lost his angel wings or his footing, and now, he was struggling to stay up, while the lightheaded Magda tugged and tugged on his ears, then, grabbing his front legs she pulled with all her might to save her savior.

The problem was, Bromista was one heavy little son of a gun. So, there they sat, for seconds, maybe minutes, face to face, with Magda pulling with all her might, Bromista scrambling with his back legs to get some kind of traction, and, unfortunately for them, this limbo was fast turning into a living hell. How long could she hold out, thought Magda.

Their eyes met. Magda knew. Bromista knew. They had to make a choice here. They were not going to be able to hold out forever. Something had to give. Magda, swearing softly, didn't want to let go of her beloved burro. But Bromista, realizing that it was either him, or both of them, softly mouthed at Magda's hands, looked her straight in the eye, and when she refused to let go, he gently bit at one hand, then the other. She still didn't let go, and finally, realizing that she wasn't catching on to his signal, or, which was more likely, he thought, the stubborn woman is going to fall to her death, he bit her hand harder. In an instant, without touching another piece of dirt until he was at the bottom of the cliff, Bromista fell head over hoof to his sure death.

Magna, watching her burro silently fall then hearing the bone-crushing thud at the bottom of the cliff, lay there with tears running down her face. Then she got up, took a look down, couldn't see hide or hair of her burro, and promptly walked back into the village.

Yes, she was glad to be alive. But the price she had paid was a dear one. A price, she thought, that she would never forgive herself for…"all," she cursed under her breath as she walked the soft sand trail back to the village, "because of that strange feeling." The feeling of being…rushed.

She promised herself, then and there, that she would never let that feeling overcome her again and that if she did feel it, she would stop everything she was doing and wait for the feeling to go away.

Back in the village, Magda hysterically bleated out her story of how she had been blindsided by a bandit and how Bromista had saved her life by flying through the air and plucking her off the cliff. Surrounded by at least ten people, they all whispered supportive words, saying what a shame it was that the burro was dead. "Que lastima…what a shame."

Magda suddenly yelled out, "I didn't say he was dead. I said I think he might be dead. I really don't know. We need to try to save him."

"Save him. He went over the cliffs. Who would want to risk their lives for a burro."

"We must save him," she yelled, turning to her son Gorde, who shrugged and whispered, "okay Mamma, okay." He turned to a few of his friends, who just shrugged back, then scurried off to give a valiant effort to save the stupid burro who, Gorde thought, if he could really fly, wouldn't be in this predicament in the first place.

At the edge of the cliff, they tied a huge rope around Gorde's waist and slowly lowered him down the face of the cliff. Near the bottom, a mangled, twisted bloody corpse of a glob sat oozing yet still.

"I see him. If he's not dead, he probably wishes that he was, que no?"

"Don't joke around Hijo," Magda said. "Is he alive?"

Gorde couldn't lie to his mother, although he thought about it for just a flash. So the burro suffers for a few more minutes, he's going to die anyway.

"Let me down a little more, that's it!"

He was now so close he could probably touch the thing, if he wanted to, which he really didn't.

"I saw his eye move. I think he's still alive. But Mama, he is in bad shape. Mama…seriously, maybe we should shoot him. I'm not kidding. Es horrible."

Magda's heart skipped a beat, "Bring him up here. Let me be the judge."

So Gorde came back up, made preparations to extract the animal. When he went back down he took a good look at the situation. Sure, Bromista was stuck right through the chest with a massive cactus spear.

But, this very same cactus, which Gorde had never seen before in his life, was probably what had allowed the burro to survive. It was a massive cactus, about twenty feet in circumference, with large pole-like flowers sticking right up into the air.

Similar to a maguey plant, it had long, lean arm-like leaves, about three inches thick and nearly fifteen feet long, which all came out from the center. And these huge leaves had been what had saved the burro's life. The ooze from the cactus coated parts of the burro with a clear green slim that made it difficult to even think about touching the burro.

Still, three hours later, with the help of half a dozen friends and some strong cable, Bromista was hauled to the top of the cliff. His blood had soaked through the large canvas tarp they had strapped to the cables to help carry him up. When Magda got her first look at him she sucked up a mouthful of air, rolled her eyes and hit the soft dirt of the trail—face first.

"Ay Chihuahua," whispered Gorde, "Now we've got two nearly dead burros to deal with."

Amidst a bit of laughter, Gorde's Mama came to, took one look at her son's face and said, "Hijo, I think we need to act fast, or he won't make it."

With that, she gave them instructions on how to get the burro down the hill, safely tucked away in the barn. They would have to leave him in the canvas, keeping all the weight off what was left of his legs.

That night, after the healer gave Bromista the once over he frowned and said, "Pretty bad. I'm afraid this burro isn't going to be worth much."

"Will he live?"

"I don't know Magda, but if he does he won't be able to carry anything. In fact, he might have a hard time with even his own weight. He has three broken shoulders, four broken legs, three of them multiple…"

As the vet listed off the injuries to Bromista, Magda thought back to when she had strained her legs and how her father had told her to put honey on it. It had been a beautiful airy spring day and she was playing around near the lagoon, trying to scare up a fish or two for dinner. She stumbled, fell, and bruised her leg, sprained her ankle. When she arrived at home, her father, a kind and gentle soul, softly coated her right foot with honey and told her it would keep the swelling down and let it heal faster. It had worked. Or, at least, the TLC from her father had worked.

"What about honey," she blurted out to the healer, who was now listing off the drugs that he thought might or might not work.

"Magda. I'm gonna tell you the truth. I don't think anything we do can really save this guy. Now, I'm not saying to kill him. But then again, he's in a lot of agony. As for honey, hell, try anything that you think will work. If he likes it, feed it to him. He's gonna need a whole lot of energy to survive this mess."

With that, the healer left, saying that when she decided which type of approach she wanted to take to give him a call. Magda, now convinced that the only way to save Bromista was with honey, called out to her family, her friends, to gather all the honey they could possibly muster up. With their help by the next morning she had close to fifty gallons of honey ready to put onto her sad little sack excuse of a burro.

Gorde, against his own desires but listening to his mother's wishes, divided one of the barn stalls in half with wood, and sealed all the cracks with tar or anything else he could get his hands on. In effect, he was building a bath for the burro to soak in.

And, soak he did, strung up by cables, with the canvas material and the honey supporting his weight, Bromista spent his days sitting in a huge bath of honey. The only part that didn't get covered was his head and tail end. After about a week of this treatment, Magda called to her son to pull the burro out and see if there was any progress. Parts of the burro, random parts, were beginning to heal, and heal rather quickly. Still, other parts looked like they were getting worse, festering.

They lowered Mista back into his tub and Gorde, up until now really was not involved emotionally in the care and feeding of the burro, suddenly had a flash of an idea. What if the parts of the burro that were healing are the same ones that were covered in cactus goo? He wasn't sure. He couldn't remember, but it could be worth it. Again, he was reluctant to mention this to his Mama, because, he knew, she would ask him to cart some of the huge cactus back to see if he was right. Probably the whole fuckin' thing, he thought, but being the son he was, he went into tell his Mom about his idea.

"Hijo…that's it. That's it," she said, and they were soon carting truckloads of the cactus back to the barn to keep Mista's bath circulating with the cactus. The thing is…it worked. And within a month the burro didn't have a scab on his body. Of course, once the news of the burro's recovery, well, kind of recovery spread, the mixture of honey and cactus was a hot item. Gorde put it on his father's shelves, right along with the tequila and mescal and sangrita. And on his off days, Gorde started to plant some of the cactus in their far field.

His father wondered out to the field one day, told Gorde that he was planting his cacti too far apart.

"No," the young man solemnly said to his father, "these plants are giant. You would not have believed it Papa. You would not have believed it."

As Mista started to feel better, it was getting harder and harder to keep him in his bath. Gorde nearly had to hog tie him every time he took him out for inspection.

"I think we can take the brace off now, " Magda said, about three months into the ordeal, "let's see how it looks."

So off came the brace. Mista's head, not quite strong enough to hold itself up, yet not so weak as not to, swayed back and forth, started to fall, then recovered, and after about five minutes of this Magda proclaimed, "I think he'll get stronger if we keep the brace off. Otherwise, his muscles will never get built up."

Course, Mista's neck muscles, along with a whole bunch of other muscles, never did quite recover.

Craig Galetas, the recently arrived surfer from Southern California who had taken an instant liking to Gorde said, "Maybe we should be feeding Mista some of that cactus juice and honey rather than soaking him in it."

"What the hell," said Gorde, "why not. I'll make up a special brew for the old bastard."

Instant success! It's the only word that can describe what happened next.

And still to this day, most people in the village who were alive during this time say it must have been the eighth wonder of the world. Gorde fed Mista one gallon of his newly produced Mescal from the giant cactus plant and bang, zoom.

Craig was out back behind Gorde's playing his guitar and drinking a little sangrita and tequila himself, and singing a little blues tune, when all of a sudden, someone from the barn joined in and let out the most incredible soul aching, gut movin' blues yell they'd ever heard. It was enough to bring James Brown back from the dead, requesting blues lessons.

It was Mista. Drunk. He had broken out of his barn/bath set-up, was singing to the moon, to the island, to the world. And, miracle of all miracles, he was standing…kinda. Swaying back and forth like a drunk, he walked his way over to the guitar playing hippie surfer who, although he was in a little shock, just kept on playing.

Gorde went to get his Mom, but she was already on the porch, looking down at her burro as he howled to the world that yes, he might be a crippled fucked up animal, but he was alive, he had spirit. The fact was he had the spirit of Gorde's new concoction and it was a strange and powerful one.

For two hours Mista, Craig, Gorde, Magda and a few other assorted friends and neighbors had an unofficial coming out party for the burro, drinking and singing. And that, as the story goes, was the beginning of a period that Craig Galetas liked to call the "broken ball blues" days.

That night, after all the people had gone home, Magda again told Gorde the story, about how Mista flew across the gully to save her life. And she told him about the feeling that she had had that started it all, the feeling of being rushed. And how she hoped that she would never have to feel that way again. And Gorde knew, that for the first time in his life, he had been a part of the history of Esmeralda. A part of a story that would probably be told for generations to come.

Chapter II

It took about half a cone of homemade nopale flavored ice cream before Martin learned more than he cared to about Stan's life and beliefs. Stan, an American expatriate, told Martin all about how he had come to the island back in 1938, (March 21, to be exact) three days after the expropriation of the U.S. oil company he had worked for in Guadalajara. He had been a salesman with about one hundred steady clients, when his job, his company, his life were expropriated by the Mexican Government. He wasn't only a twenty-five year old foreigner out of a job, he was nearly out a life.

He had been coming home from work on a warm spring day, eating pistachio ice cream, when he heard the news on the radio and immediately turned around toward his office. When he arrived, sure enough, soldiers surrounded the fenced off compound. He tried to talk his way back in to get a few personal things like pictures of his family back home, and his sports coat and most importantly of all, his paycheck, that sat in the right hand drawer of his desk. After a lengthy argument, which at times got a little heated, Stan backed down momentarily.

"If the schmuck didn't have a gun strapped over his shoulder", Stan recalled, "I'd have given him a left hook to end all."

But they did have the guns, the uniforms, and the power and Stan was out of luck. Angry, frustrated and suddenly unemployed, he went out with a couple of his other co-workers to the local cantina to discuss their situation. Five beers later Stan came up with a plan to sneak back into the office. Three out of the four other guys were game, since they all had their paychecks sitting in their desks. Only Henry, a whiny, scared little boy in a man's body, didn't want to go, because he reasoned…"they're the government."

This actually helped the others to get up their nerve to go through with the escapade. Even though Stan had only lived in Mexico for a couple of years, he had a healthy, all-Mexican hatred of the government, and this current crisis was helping to cement a hatred he would have burning in his stomach for the rest of his life.

So the four of them waited until dark, and snuck back in, gathered up their personal belonging and checks and headed out the back way. Everything would have been fine, except for Henry, the one who hadn't wanted to go, had decided that he wanted to get his stuff after all, and went back to the front side of the compound. Henry was in a full blown argument about his belongings, when he spotted the gang sneaking out of the building and inadvertently tipped their hands by looking their way. The guard, catching a glimpse of the culprits and thinking that Henry had been arguing with him all along just to distract him, handcuffed Henry to the fence, sounded an alarm, and flashed a dull flash light in the direction of Stan and his three partners in crime.

Stan and his friends popped over the fence and were ready for a clean getaway, when they saw that Henry was cuffed to the fence. Stan told his friends to keep on keepin' on, he'd meet them back at the Cantina, he was going to get Henry. They argued for a moment, but when Stan basically ordered them to go, they complied.

So Stan went back, trying to get Henry off the hook and promptly got shot in the leg. It wasn't a big wound, at least it didn't look that way, but it sure hurt, and it had ripped right through the front part of his thigh, shredding the muscles and cracking his bone.

Both Stan and Henry were carted off to jail, where they sat for a good three months before their company, or what was left of it in

Mexico, figured out how to bribe them out. But the damage had been done. Stan would never be able to run again, and was lucky enough to be able to walk free of pain. And his hate of the Mexican government was cemented into his psyche like the artifacts in Esmeralda's city hall.

Another source of Stan's anger were the visions he had of playing professional baseball somewhere, even in the winter leagues. This dream, along with his boyish exuberance for life itself, faded away in his small jail cell. So it was a bitter, angry and broke Stan who when freed took off for a nearly deserted island to live out the rest of his life as a hermit.

Stan found himself in the town of Esmeralda when the town was about the size of Hermana, the small village on the far side of the island. Both Hermana and Esmeralda sported a population of less than five hundred. He had wanted to be alone, so he found himself a location outside of Esmeralda, about a mile or two, and proceeded to build a palapa out of palm fronds.

He did a pretty good job of adjusting, except for the intense cravings for ice cream and a good professional baseball game. "Just cause I can't play it anymore," he'd mutter, "doesn't mean I can't watch it."

So at least once a month, Stan would leave his little island paradise, take the boat to the mainland, and find a hotel room with American TV and watch a game. It was a luxury he could ill afford, since he hadn't worked for years, and he usually spent his whole disability check on his two or three day trips to town. But for Stan, it was well worth it.

One day, after being on the island for nearly three years, Stan was limping home from one of his excursions when he saw a vision from the heavens. A strikingly beautiful Indian woman came walking up the path, pushing a cart of some kind. Her hair was long and black and tied back in two braided, beautiful red-ribboned trails of majesty. Dressed in the traditional multi-colored hand-woven dress of Hermana, she took his breath away.

Stan stopped, stared, let his jaw open so wide he could have drooled all over the dirt if it wasn't for his cottonmouth. He felt his heart race when she looked at him with her calm and friendly dark brown eyes. By now, Stan knew a little Spanish and he gave the traditional hello he had heard over the years. She answered back, and he nearly dropped to his knees. A voice from the heavens, he thought, what more could a man ask for?

When she pulled to within five feet of him, thinking that maybe he wanted to buy some of her goods; Stan looked down at the sign on her cart and fainted. Like a cut timber, he fell to the ground, luckily landing on the soft dirt. When he came to, she was dabbing his face with a damp towel.

"Senor, Senor. Are you okay?"

Stan looked at her beauty, it was still there. Slowly, he turned and stared at the cart, and yes, he hadn't been hallucinating, the sign read, "Helado"—ice cream.

"Would you like some?" the woman asked.

Stan stayed down on the ground, waiting for his head to clear, still not sure what happened, still not believing that he was seeing this beautiful woman and ice cream all in one fell swoop.

"Might as well bump into Babe Ruth while I'm at it," he whispered. He sat on the ground while the woman scooped up a bit of ice cream and put it into a banana leaf. When she came back to him, she had made one for herself too. They sat, in near silence, while they enjoyed the ice cream. Stan, trying to get a hold of himself, tried not to look at her eyes too much, or her dress, or her, period. He knew some time or another he was going to have to get up off of the ground and he didn't want to end up back in the dirt.

"This is incredible," Stan moaned in Spanish, as he ate the smooth, silky ice cream, "What flavor is this?"

"It's my own special recipe, that has been in the family for generations. It's nopales."

Stan just looked at her, he was still a little dizzy, asking, "Nopales?"

"Cactus" she said, in English.

"You speak English?"

"Just a little. I had neighbors from Canada for two year. They taught me."

"It's very good. Thank you," Stan said in English. "I'm Stan."

"Nancy."

After he was done they sat and talked in Spanish for a good ten minutes and Stan asked her if he could come by and get more ice cream sometime in the near future. Nancy didn't come this way very often because she usually sold her ice cream on the streets of Hermana.

"That would be a long walk with a cart like that," Stan said as he stood up for the first time.

"Usually," Nancy said, pointing off into the jungle, "I use the old trails, but they were pretty cold this morning so I decided to take the road. And I'm glad I did."

Stan felt his knees wobble. What a smile, he thought. And, she likes me.

It was the beginning of a courtship that would last for a full two years. Nothing moves fast on the island, and Stan, as well as Nancy, didn't want to rush into anything. But over the months, Nancy taught Stan how to make ice cream island style, and Stan, in his friendly yet insistent way taught Nancy the finer points of baseball.

When they started going to the mainland together to see games and Nancy loved the sport, Stan was a goner and wedding bells could be heard between the cheers at the stadium. Over the years they found that most of their ice cream was sold in Esmeralda, so they moved their cart, and their kids, and their belonging to the then outskirts of town and settled into a modest palapa.

What happened next is another one of the mysteries of Esmeralda, because over the years, the town seemed to crowd around Stan and Nancy's little palapa, like people sometimes congregate in a kitchen during a party. Some say it was the ice cream, which was the heart and soul of Esmeralda. Others say that the upper side of the hill, with a beautiful view of the lagoon, was the prime real estate in the city and yet others, said Stan was the heart and soul of Esmeralda, so why not be the heart of town. Whatever the case, the town came to them, and Stan and Nancy, not wanting to move again, stayed put, living much like they had been living in the old days, with a palapa with no doors and just a couple of dividers to keep out the dust.

They pretty much kept to themselves, with Stan only having occasional run-in's with the government (he still despised governments of any type, even small town institutions), and that was where things stood one morning when Stan heard about the newly instituted property taxes.

Esmeralda's property tax rebellion started about five years after city hall was built. When the Federal building money ran out, Adelante, thinking he could raise a few dollars for the city, put a tax on property. He posted signs all over town telling the fair citizens of Esmeralda that every building on the island, once it was complete, would have to pay a few pesos in taxes, based on the building's value.

"That's the most ridiculous thing I've ever heard of," Stan yelled, still young and full of vigor. "He can't do that. He just can't do that. How do you know how much a building is worth. Who will have pesos to even pay the tax? He's out of his mind. I won't do it. I won't."

Frothing and angry, Stan stomped down to city hall as fast as his good leg would take him, told Adelante his idea for a property tax was "the most ridiculous idea he'd ever heard" and that if he didn't rescind it, there was going to be trouble. The Mayor, calmly replying to Stan's anger, told Stan that only cement buildings would be taxed, native style palapas would not be taxed, "So relax Stan. You won't have to pay."

This made Stan even angrier.

First, he thought maybe the Mayor was just trying to bribe him so he wouldn't create trouble, but then, after he read the announcement that the Mayor had handed him while he was getting the "good news" that he didn't have to pay, Stan saw a flaw in the document. The law only applied to completed buildings.

"So this is it," Stan said. "This is the law. It can't be changed."

"Yup," Adelante happily told him, "it's in cement, like the artifacts. Look, palapas and other native buildings do not have to pay the tax. Paragraph 5, line 2."

"Can I keep this?" Stan sheepishly asked.

"Sure," Adelante said, "post one in your shop if you want."

As Stan walked away, he read and re-read the announcement and looked at the sentence on paragraph 8, line 2, that said, "this tax shall apply to all completed properties that use cement as their main building material."

All completed properties, thought Stan, so if it's not completed, then it can't be taxed. He set out to test the law, thinking it might be nice to have a small addition to his palapa, made out of blocks and cement and re-bar. So, the following day, Stan and few of his friends started to build the small building right next to his palapa. "A cold-storage area," he told Adelante when he questioned him, and also questioned why he wanted to build a cement building, now that it would get taxed.

"That's why I was so interested the other day," Stan calmly said, "Because I knew I would have to use cement and block to keep the ice cream cold. We have to expand and this is the only way. Progress, you know."

The mayor smiled at Stan, not really sure he was hearing correctly, and walked away shaking his head in wonder, mumbling, "My God, has Stan finally seen the light?"

Three weeks later, with the cold-storage nearly done, except for the top part, that sported various pieces of re-bar sticking out like the antennae of a Martian, Stan told his friends to go home, they were done. "Thanks guys, I'll take it from here."

Henry Ortiz, who was assigned by Adelante to check on construction projects and follow the new law to a tee, showed up to assess the value of Stan's new addition.

"Well Henry, it's not quite done yet," Stan began, "but someday, it'll be done, I'm sure."

Henry, not realizing that Stan had no intention of ever finishing the building, stepped back, took an admiring look at the building and said, "It'll be nice when it's done. It's the first building I've had to assess. I'll make sure it's low for you, Stan. You are a good man. How about another ice cream?"

"Sure," Stan said. And three weeks later, when Henry came back, and the building wasn't done, Stan offered Henry another free ice cream, "Why don't you try our new chocolate Henry? I think you'll like it."

"Okay," Henry said, then, "Stan, when do you think you're going to finish this building?"

"Henry, to be honest with you, I don't know. I could be a long time. A long, long time," Stan cooed with a wry smile.

This time, Henry had gotten the message and when he reported back to Adelante that Stan was not finishing the building, so he couldn't tax him, Adelante told him to assess it unfinished.

So Henry, knowing that Stan wouldn't like this bit of news, and trying to keep the peace, went back to Stan's and told him, "Listen, Stan, we're going assess your property unfinished and then, when you finish it, I'll probably have to come back and assess it again. So why don't you just finish it off this week, I'll come back, do my job, and we can call it quits. What do you say?"

What followed isn't suitable for print, not alone the ears of Stan's kids. Nancy, trying to calm him down, actually put a double-scoop macadamia nut cone right into his mouth, nearly choking him.

But Stan was not to be stopped, he ranted and raved through the ice cream and finally calmed down enough that some of the people who were still left understood him, which wasn't Henry, by the way, because he had left about ten minutes into the tirade.

"We'll have a Boston Tea Party!" Stan screamed. "Hasn't that stupid Pargo heard about the Boston Tea Party!"

When Stan was sent a property tax bill, he promptly and proudly displayed it behind his counter, like some establishments display their first dollar bill. And every year, when his bill came, he put it up behind the counter, and didn't pay it.

Of course, word got out and poor Henry, who was just trying to do his job, couldn't collect a cent in taxes. Everyone had caught on to Stan's silent revolution. Gorde Tranquilleno's, when he added on to his liquor store, had at least a dozen hunks of re-bar sticking out the top, covered with old tequila bottles, some of them actually antique, which could probably be sold for a pretty penny.

The Hotel Esmeralda itself, in which Adelante was part owner, had re-bar sticking out the top. "If they aren't going to pay, why should I," he said to Henry the tax collector when asked to contribute.

"Adelante, how could you?" Henry responded.

But even the church had its re-bar sticking out from the top. After Adelante's choice to leave re-bar on his hotel he changed the tax procedures, recognizing that he couldn't really collect on his bills, he now sent out "building in progress" notices, with the expected tax to be collected once the building was done.

And that was why, every building on the island which was made out of cement, to this very day, had a few pieces of re-bar sticking out the top. The tax collector still walked the streets, writing on his report, "Building in progress." And that was also why the city of Esmeralda had never, ever collected a dime in property taxes—thanks to Stan and Nancy Lovejoy.

As the years passed by, the couple grew older, and now, many, many, years later, they still had the original cart out front, holding up their sign. It still bore the original ice cream recipe that melted Stan's heart back in the old days. And the original property tax bills, now old and yellow, some not even legible, hung proudly behind the register.

Sure, some things had changed. Conchita and Stan Junior were now exporting the honey-flavored ice cream to the mainland. It was something that Nancy had been against at first, but agreed to it after it was decided that it would be a good way to keep their kids ON the island and not moving to the mainland like many of the others.

Stan and Nancy, now both pushing eighty and spending a good part of their days in hammocks, relaxing and enjoying the fruits of their labor, were happy with things just the way they were, thank you. Then Stan heard about how the Mayor had dropped his little "Black Sands Resort" bomb on the village.

"We should hang the fucking Pargo by his balls," he yelled out from his hammock, waving his cane at the sky while Nancy shushed him and told him the grandkids were listening. And they were, wide-eyed and excited, knowing that something big was about to happen in the village.

"That little Pargo nosed son-of-a-bitch won't get away with this. No sir!"

It was war thought Stan. It might be his last one. He was going to make it a worthwhile one.

And Martin Slate, finishing up his second cone of the day, sat in the shady hammock and wondered what the hell he had accidentally ignited and whether he should get off the island before heads started to roll.

Chapter 12

For Magdelena Sanchez Tranquilleno, time was never of the essence. If she were to read a modern-day real estate contract with the words, "time is of the essence" splattered across the page, she probably would have lit it on fire. The only day in her life she ever rushed was the day she fell off the cliff and was saved by her burro Bromista.

As she grew older and older, her "time thing" as her son Gorde referred to it, became stronger and stronger. She didn't like to think about time, except in the old way. Which is to say, she didn't like to think about time.

"In the old days," she liked to mumble, "a year was a short period of time and we really, most of the time, didn't count years. These days, everybody is in a rush."

Many thought Magda's time thing was the reason she threw limes at people who wore watches, but nobody really knew for sure. Gorde repeatedly asked his mother why she threw the limes (although he thought he knew why) and over the years she had given him a whole bunch of reasons, none of them making much sense.

"What else have I got to do?" or "Because the people ask for it, que no, wearing those time pieces on their wrists," flinching when she said the words, "time pieces" and even one time, which had given Gorde his clue, she had said, "Better than bullets. Que no?"

Gorde had his theory. Once he had read about a deranged man in Mexico City who made a habit of asking passerby the time, just like his aged mother. But this man, a little sicker than Magda, and definitely more serious about his relationship with time, would shoot the people who were wearing watches—no questions asked. Gorde thought, somehow, his mom had gotten a hold of this information one day, in fact, maybe that's where he had read it, and she had filed it in her subconscious to be used when she was old and in reality, had nothing much else to do.

So Gorde, in one sense, was glad his Mom was just throwing harmless, used up lime halves at people. It was a lot less bloody than the man from Mexico City and only occasionally caused a fallout, which Gorde had to admit, were sometimes kinda fun.

There was the time Magda tossed a lime at Craig Galetas and his monkey as they walked off the verandah in front of Gorde's liquor store. Craig didn't even flinch. He had been hit by a few limes in his time, and with the state of his clothes, he never really noticed if he had a lime stain or some other kind of stain. But for Mickey the monkey, this was his first experience with Magda's lime vengeance. When the lime bounced off Craig's back and splashed limejuice in the monkey's eye, he went berserk.

Before the lime hit the ground, Mickey turned on Magna, jumped on her back, screaming and yelling and hissing into her ear. Then, much to everyone's consternation, Mickey bit the bottom part of Magda's wrinkled ear lobe, clean off and proceeded to chew on it like a gummy bear.

Craig Galetas, fearing for Magda's life, came running to the rescue. But two steps was all he could take before Magda, not clear about what was going on and thinking she was under attack, promptly kicked Craig squarely in the balls. As Craig dropped to his knees in pain, Magda flipping Mickey off her back, grabbed him by his left arm, right at the wrist, and swung him around like a huge, plucked turkey. Suddenly stopping after three swings, and going against the momentum, she flipped

Mickey's wrist, making the same, flat sudden pop, pop sound turkeys had made for Magda for many, many years when she had skillfully broken their necks.

Gorde, who had been in the bathroom during to all this, came out tucking in his shirt to see pandemonium and yelled at the top of his lungs, "STOP!"

Magda, Mickey and Craig all froze for a moment; like a bunch of kids caught with their hands in the tortilla drawer. Then, all at once, as if Gorde's body movement was conducting them, started to scream at Gorde.

Simultaneously: Magda told her son that she nearly died during the attack, that this "fucking monkey was chewing on her ears like popcorn, and that she was going to go get her gun and take care of all of them, if he didn't go for the gun, right now! Craig complained that his balls were still lost somewhere inside his abdomen, probably near his bellybutton and that Magda should try out for the American football league as a kicker; and that if he didn't get some tequila in him, hopefully with a little bit of cactus juice, he was going to die…of pain. And Mickey, he just sat on the ground holding his broken wrist in the air, screaming at the top of his lungs, and wishing he had the energy to bite the other ear off the deranged old bitch.

"Ay Carumba, nobody move. Okay. Just nobody move," Gorde whistled, then he gathered up four tall glasses and poured tequila in them, with a splash of cactus juice and filled four smaller glasses with sangrita.

Three hours later, drunk and painless, somehow the problem had been solved. Mickey's wrist was reset and wrapped and would probably heal just fine. Craig's balls had dropped down like a newborn's, although they would remain swollen and black and blue for two weeks. Magda's anger had subsided and she even admitted maybe Craig wasn't part of the attack (she still kept her distance from "his crazy monkey") and her ear, covered in a thick half-inch coating of honey, had finally stopped bleeding. All was well.

So, yes, it was true that sometimes Magda's lime throwing had created problems, but on the whole, nobody really cared too much about her habit. And most people, when asked what time it was, even if they knew, simply said, "I don't know." Which made Magda feel good enough not to toss a lime, and let the person off the hook without too much effort.

Chapter 13

"De lo dicho, a lo hecho, hay mucho trecho"

As each person learned about the resort, and thought about its possible impact on the island, it was akin to lining up sticks of dynamite, intertwining them together with one huge fuse, then waiting for someone to light the fuse. The scary part was, the Island of Esmeralda was known for having a very, very short fuse.

For instance, back in 1964 the town of Esmeralda showed off its lack of patience, or lack of negotiation skills or lack of plain common sense when they had an incident commonly referred to as the "Taxi Slaughters."

The town had Two taxi companies that serviced it; the green-topped VW's called Central Taxi, and the freelance company Reliable, that sported white topped roofs on all of its cars (these cars were just about anything that could hold white paint on its roof). All in all, they both did a pretty good business, with the town divided into sections, and each company having its own "territories." Central's main territory seemed to be the dock, probably to make a good first impression on visitors, and Reliable usually handled the downtown section. Then assorted smaller sections of town were equally divided into mini-territories. It was a pretty happy arrangement that kept both companies alive in lean times and prosperous otherwise.

But in the summer of 1964 this all came to an abrupt end. The problems started when a driver for Reliable, Pedro Escobar, picked up a fare off of Surfer Beach. Reliable didn't have the contract for this part of town.

Pedro, in his usual drunken stupor, thought he was on the other side of the island and grabbed the rider, right in front of three green-topped competitors.

The green-topped Central drivers at first gave their horns a small toot, figuring the Reliable Driver would relinquish. But Pedro, hearing the horns, ushered his fare into his barely running vehicle and gave all three drivers the bird, along with a few choice words like, "Why don't you get on your side of the fuckin' island," or something to that effect.

The green-topped drivers, who liked to think of themselves as fairly civil as well as professional individuals, all simultaneously put their right feet on their horns (which was a peculiar horn blowing technique used on the island) and, with a cacophony of horns blasting so loud you couldn't hear a space shuttle lift off, stood out their windows and yelled a few choice words back at the poor, confused Pedro.

Pedro promptly backed into the nearest green-top, knocking the drivers foot off his horn and his glasses off his face, and sped off, wondering why all those green-tops were so far away from home.

Word travels fast on the island. Within half an hour green-topped cabs were picking up passengers in downtown. Fights started to break out and general havoc ensued. It was a night to remember, with more than one passenger wondering why his cab was being commandeered off the road by another cab driver.

What happened next, who did it first, and why it happened was and forever will be impossible to figure. Some people think it was years of pent up anger and aggression suddenly freed to run its course. Other just shake their head and say, "It's the island, what do you expect?"

Whatever the case the "Taxi Slaughters", as they were dubbed, had officially began.

The following night, and night after night, week after week, and month after month, taxi drivers were found on the beach: maimed, knocked out, blinded and sometimes, dead. Throats slit, heads crushed, arms mutilated—all because of an innocent mistake, that most people, as the days passed by, didn't even remember.

In fact, a popular topic in town was, "How did this get started?" and "How can we stop it?"

After awhile it had been going on so long that neither side remembered why they were fighting. Even the chief of police was getting tired of the situation.

The then chief of police, Gonzalo Perchino, had decided, like most chiefs of police on the island usually ended up deciding, that it was best for his men to stay clear of the nonsense and let the crazies fight it out.

"We will not put up with any foul play," Gonzalo told anyone who would listen, "and that is that! We won't stand for it!"

Gonzalo figured if he talked a good game, he would look good and not lose his job. So daily he was interviewed on the local radio station stating his strong position. And every now and again another body was found on the Surfer's Beach, with a note attached to their toe like an I.D. tag in the morgue.

Within three months the "Taxi Slaughters" had taken their toll; three dead, five blinded so they could never drive again, and a dozen other men with missing fingers, hands and arms. The town was littered with women walking around in black mourning dresses.

Chief Gonzalo was becoming a nervous wreck, with bloody fingers, nails half bitten off, black rings under his swollen sleep deprived eyes, and, miracle of all miracles, his belt buckle three notches up.

"If this is what it take for me to lose weight, I don't want any of it," he thought one night while he paced his living room floor at three a.m., then stopped to tighten his belt yet another notch.

He frantically upped his propaganda messages, using a small pick-up truck with a huge speaker. He had his deputies drive around the town spewing out his message. "We will not put up with any more killings. It must stop. Now!"

No investigations. No forensics. No one listened. "De lo dicho, a lo hecho, hay mucho trecho", roughly translated means, "Between what is said, and what is done, there is a lot of distance."

Finally, when the death toll hit ten the women of the town called a strike. They would walk to the market on Saturday and Wednesday. They would walk to church on Sunday and cards on Monday. But they would not take another taxi. Not until the craziness was over.

Business fell off, and even so, the owners of the two taxi services were having a hard time finding drivers to cover their needs. Many of the regular drivers quit, in fear for their lives. Replacements were hard to find. And the replacements found were more interested in the fights than the fares. Being a driver was now becoming a "legal" way to get even with someone who had done you wrong, say, ten years ago. Just sign up for the opposing side's staff, then pick up a fare right in front of that person's cab. A fight would begin. Then, if the person was found dead on the beach the next day, well…it was business.

Paulo Gabernetti, the owner of Reliable, and Vicente Fernandez, the owner of Central, were both losing so many drivers that they were about to go bankrupt. Both men, in their early forties, had much to lose. They had been in the business for over twenty years, built up a good little two man monopoly of the Island taxi services and didn't want to give it all up because of one drunk's mistake. They both also knew they had absolutely no control over their cabbies. Even Vicente, who prided himself in being in control of his business "empire" knew this truth.

Paulo, the son of an Italian fisherman who had immigrated to the Island years ago, was terrified of having to be a fisherman. All he had to do was think about one day out on the ocean and his stomach twisted and turned and he ended up on his living room floor in great pain. He hated the water so much it made him sick. He even had a hard time eating fish because it reminded him of the ocean. So, Paulo, one night sitting on his balcony watching the fishermen go out for their midnight run that would last way into the morning, decided that he had to find a way out of this mess.

He didn't know what it was, but he was going to break the ice, try to get a truce going before he was forced back into the boats.

Vicente Fernandez, on the other hand, had come from a long line of wealthy mainland taxi company owners. His position was firm. His grandfather and his father were both calling him on a daily basis, telling him to hang tough, this was how family fortunes were made and lost. Stay strong, don't give in, was their message and Vicente believed them.

To a man they didn't like the violence, but to a man they agreed that business was business was business. Vicente would have to hold strong and prevail.

That's why, three days later when both men came together trying to figure out an agreement on how the "Taxi Slaughters" were to come to an end, it was almost a miracle. Paulo had approached Vicente at his morning coffee shop on Surfer Beach.

He didn't know exactly what to say, but it probably didn't matter, because whatever he would have tried to say Vicente surely wouldn't have listened. But before Paulo could sputter a word, an irate ex-driver, who had been sipping on a coconut spiked with rum for about three hours, came rushing out of the bushes toward Vicente's back, welding a two foot long machete. The ex-driver didn't make a noise. But Paulo, acting instinctively, brushed Vicente aside and drop kicked the crazed intruder right in the chest with his special karate-style kick he had perfected over the years during bar brawls.

Over ten people had witnessed the event. Angel, who worked the coffee shop, said at first he thought Vicente's number was up and that he felt it was strange that Paulo, who had obviously put a hit out on

Vicente's life, would be so stupid as to stand there and watch the whole event.

Angel had thought maybe Paulo was there to watch, to make sure everything went right, or maybe, Angel surmised, Paulo was a "sick mother-fucker with a death wish", and wanted to let everyone on the island know that he was responsible for the hit.

But finally, Angel had surmised, Paulo just didn't want to get his hands dirty with the actual act of killing Vicente. Then, when Paulo dropkicked the worker, Angel had thought, things had really gotten screwed up. "Que confusion!"

But besides Angel's little bit of conjecture, which was truly put to rest within a few minutes, it was one of the few times on the island where everyone agreed on something: Paulo had saved Vicente's life.

The ramifications of this truth were especially hard to swallow for Vicente. Once the police carried off the crazed machete-wielding worker, Vicente had time to think about what had happened and realized he could have been a dead man. He looked over to Paulo, who by now was calmly sipping on his second cup of coffee, and realized something had to give. Against the wishes of the Fernandez Empire and probably against his better judgment, Vicente walked over and quietly sat down for a cup of coffee with Paulo.

Paulo, who had actually enjoyed showing off his drop kick, now realized that by saving Vicente's life, he had also earned his ear. So, over a casual cup of coffee, they agreed to talk. Small talk. Nothing of substance. Paulo gave Vicente a rough estimation of his numbers, and how bad they were. Vicente did the same. Both men lied about their numbers. But it didn't matter, because they soon realized, even though they had been arch rivals for the last twenty or so years, they had a lot in common. Still, they couldn't come up with a way to stop the killing. They needed a way to solve the problem and save face. Three cups of coffee later, with no solution, they agreed to meet again; this time for a drink. Maybe a little stronger fuel would inspire them to find a solution.

For weeks, the pair could be seen in every bar on the island. Still, the fighting and killing went on, even while the owners sat and talked, and drank, and struggled to find a solution, men were getting maimed not more than half a mile away.

After three weeks the pair did agree on one thing, they would start buying their own booze. This drinking in bars was getting expensive, night after night.

So, they went to Hector Tranquilleno's liquor store to buy a bottle of his home made tequila and, of course, a bottle of his homemade sangrita. On their way out they glanced up at a poster. The festival was coming to town. Rodeo. Parades. Cockfights.

After looking at the poster for over thirty seconds the two men's eyes met, both saw dollar signs in each other's pupils. The festival meant lots of demand for cabs. It was the eleventh hour. They needed a solution.

That night, after finishing a bottle of tequila and Hector's sangrita they came up with a solution. It was an agreement both men found not only amiable, but, in the end they commented, as they drunkenly shook hands, creative and quite a bit of fun. A cockfight would determine who got which section of town. And it was decided that the event would be a yearly tradition, because, about every year or so, they both admitted, everyone might forget who or why the sections had been divided up and that would lead to problems, maybe more bloodshed. The cockfights would be a good chance for the loser's drivers to get even or at least blow off a tremendous amount of steam, without hurting any of the competition's drivers.

So it was decided that every year during the local festival, when the taxi business was at its peak, the annual fights, which were soon dubbed the "Taxi & Tequila" fights, would be held.

Tequila and Taxi fights would have been a better description. Every year, Paulo, Vicente and their workers, who came to the fights, had so much riding on that one cockfight they tended to get a little drunk. Make that a lot drunk.

And, of course, in typical island tradition, the winner gloated and the loser accused the winner of cheating. But, also in typical and lucky island fashion, no one was killed. And every year, the women of Esmeralda were thankful for the little things.

Chapter 14

The Esmeralda Land Bureau was housed right inside City Hall, not more than ninety feet from mayor Adelante's office, even though it was not an officially sanctioned branch of Adelante's unofficial government. The ELB, as the letterhead read, was often referred to by the locals as the "Esmeralda Land Baron's Association."

The office was a strange mix of public, private and corporate interests. Originally concocted to fulfill the wishes of Adelante to appraise property (when he enacted his ill fated property tax bill), the ELB had of late evolved more into an extension of Alfredo Lopez Ramos, the sleazy real estate developer who would stoop to any means to make his buck.

Alfredo Lopez Ramos had used the office, along with Henry Ortiz, the sole employee, to propagate the Land Certificate Program, which aimed at stealing all the land from the people of Esmeralda. His scheme, in a way worked. Except for one flaw. The mainland didn't sanction the office and if the Mexican Government ever found out that Adelante, along with his friend Alfredo, had attempted a legal land grab or to collect taxes without their involvement…Adelante would be in a whole lot of trouble, to say the least.

But Adelante knew his people and they rarely left Esmeralda. When they did it was for the garage sales of Mexico City and then right back, unless of course, they were one of the lucky few that had inadvertently discovered a fortune. When people had money, they left the island, because, in reality, money wasn't much good on Esmeralda. So, Adelante was pretty sure his secret was safe.

As the sole employee, Henry Ortiz had it made at the ELB. His job mostly entailed going around and drinking coffee with his friends. He'd look up at their homes, checking to make sure they hadn't inadvertently finished off their building. When he found the unfinished re-bar sticking out, he relaxed, asked them when they were going to finish the project, and his friends gave the standard assortment of answers: "Don't have the money." "Maybe next week." "Haven't decided how many stories we want to go up."

He would then enjoy their company, talking about the bees, the fishing, assorted rumors. And he loved the fact that he got paid for this…it was his ticket out of the fishing boats, which he really didn't mind either, but sleeping in until the sunrise was nice.

The only pressure he had, and it was self-imposed, was that he wasn't really sure what he would do if someone had the nerve to finish off his or her building. In fact, every time he had to check Stan's Ice Cream, his bowels rumbled, his heart beat the rumba, his brain felt fuzzy—like he was on some sort of anesthesia. He would nervously hand over the sweat stained receipt, destined for Stan's back wall, and walk out of the store relieved that he had another year of freedom.

Chapter 15

While half the village was sharpening its machetes and obsessing over the possibility of the Black Sands Resort, ex-surfer Craig Galetas was tuning his guitar and hoping for a crowd—a tipping crowd.

He'd been on the island for over thirty years, an old-time California surfer known and loved by all for his mellow attitude and laid back approach to life. Living in a modest open-air hut called a palapa south of the Surfer's Beach, Craig grew his own food in an organic garden. He had coconuts, mangos and papayas growing so fast on his property, he had to sell leftovers to the market, and, all in all, spent his days in a relaxed stupor.

Right now, he was on "stage," tuned and ready to play some music, hoping for some tips, when he heard the news about his beach, his secret spot and he knew he had to do something about it. For the first time in a long time, he cared about something. It was a strange feeling for a man who had spent the later part of his life working hard not to care about anything whatsoever.

"It's gotta be Blackie's," he whispered to himself, "I wonder if the dude with the mask is still alive. If he is, I owe him big time."

It was true. He did owe him big time. About twenty-five years back, when Craig was young and strong and still riding the massive waves on the other side of the island, he had discovered another secret spot, that rarely broke, but when it did, it was amazing. Absolutely no one but himself knew about this break, as far as he knew.

He had discovered it by mistake one day when his boat engine, which always seemed to be about on the blink, finally closed its eyes and shut down. He drifted, and drifted. He wasn't too concerned. He always carried plenty of food and water and he knew the island pretty well. He had been surfing "the backside" as the few people who even knew about this side of the island called it, for over five years.

So while he rebuilt his carburetor, or at least tried to, he drifted into a part of the island he had never really explored before. He recognized the cliffs, the dark ones that seemed a little higher than the rest of the island. To Craig, it seemed like it was a piece of the mainland that had just broken off, so many, many years ago, and here it was, the missing piece of the puzzle. But he had always just buzzed by in his skiff, never really seeing very many waves. And besides, he didn't spend much time on this side of the island in the winter.

This time was different. Even before he saw them, he heard them. It's off season, thought Craig, that can't be surf. But it was, on the backside of the island, during the dry season and the backs of the waves must have been ten maybe fifteen feet high.

The temptation was much too much for Craig. He oared his way into the bay for a better look at the waves and when he turned back and saw the first set, it took his breath away. Pitching out tunnels so big you could drive rush hour traffic on the Santa Monica Freeway through it, Craig could feel adrenaline pumping through his veins.

After searching for five years, at last he'd found it. This was his wave. No one out with huge walls with just enough time to make it down the line. He anchored his boat, waxed down his board and paddled into the water. The paddle was a good half-mile into the area where he could actually take off on the wave. Once there, he positioned himself on the last wave of the set, took the long, fast drop to the bottom, turned into the tunnel and hung on for life. It was the tube of a lifetime. Clear, green water, so thin you could look through it and see the black cliffs blasting by. He rode another, then another and when the tide dropped, he didn't take notice, he was so excited about the waves he was getting.

There was a lull for about ten minutes and then the biggest set of the day came pounding through. Craig, deciding he wanted to take off behind the peak this time and see if he could drive through rush hour traffic at 100 miles a hour without getting caught, paddled in behind the peak and took off. He didn't even make it down the face of the wave. In fact, his body and board flew through the air and were airborne for a good three seconds before they landed in a jumble of powerful whitewater and coral. Craig heard a snap—and thought it was his board or his back. And when he popped up on the water's surface, the pain was so bad he lost consciousness for a moment. Then he came to, grabbed his back and thought it was just cut or was it? He wasn't sure. He drifted off into a state of dreamy coma for what seemed like an eternity.

The next thing Craig remembered a man wearing a strange looking multi-colored grass mask was helping him into his boat. Barely coming to when the man threw him into his boat and turned to jump into the water, Craig caught a glimpse of his eyes. He would never forget those eyes. Dark, brown, warm, caring, and a little scared. Neither man had said a word. "Shit," Craig had thought, "who was that? What was that?" The man had saved his life. Craig scanned the water and all he could see was the mask, mysteriously gliding across the water around the bend.

After eating a few crackers, drinking some water, Craig managed to get his engine back together and sputtered back to the main fishing bay. There the locals, who kept asking him what happened, helped him. He never told anyone about the man or the waves at "Blackie's". It was his little secret.

Now he sat at the hotel Esmeralda's bar, listening to the chatter. He realized what the short man with the pockmarked face was blabbering about was the masked man on the far side of the beach who had saved his life so many years ago.

Of course, thought Craig, this guy looks pretty drunk and he doesn't look very together. Maybe it's just a coincidence?" Craig took another look at the man who had just told a story about the Black Sand Beach on the other side of the island. His shoes were old and scuffed. He was not a high roller, that was for sure. And, he was talking to Lucia. Probably trying to impress her, thought Craig, but still, where would he get a story like that? He knew the island grapevine would provide him with an answer.

Chapter 16

It didn't take long for Craig Galetas to learn from the grapevine that, yes, it had been his beach "Blacks" where the incident had taken place, and, yes indeed, the man with the mask was still alive. There was going to be a big meeting at Stan's to discuss the problem. Craig wasn't sure if he wanted to get involved.

Craig, even though he was pushing fifty, had a habit of using his "flyin' machine" as he called it, to help him relax, to help him think, and to help him get a little rush out of life. It was a habit he had developed from the old days, when life got him down, he had escaped into the surf.

Now, even though he was well over two hundred pounds, even though his once blond hair was falling out, turning gray, even though his skin (which had taken the full power of the sun since he was ten) was leathery and wrinkled, Craig still used something similar to surfing to find his sanity. He liked the rush of flying. It took him up, up and away from all the worries of the real world. It gave him perspective.

His flying machine was a parasail with a few metal bars fashioned into a seat of sorts and a high-powered fan with an efficient engine that could run for a full forty-five minutes on one-half gallon of gas. When he was in the air, it was almost surrealistic. One wondered not only how he could stay up there but if he could actually steer the damn thing. But over the years he had gotten rather good at flying his "Flyin' Machine" and for Esmeraldian's it really wasn't such a strange sight.

Lately he had taken to launching it off the top of the Hotel Esmeralda, using the flat, cement roof and his rollerblades (imported from sunny California by a friend) to literally roll into the wind. The combination of the on-shore wind, the lift of the fan blowing full blast and Craig's deft handling of his flying machine allowed him to soar high above the waves.

And so, this morning when the grapevine had confirmed that his beach was the center of the conflict and the man who had literally saved his life so many years ago was still alive. He felt like he needed to do something, he needed to get above the ground and do some serious thinking.

Craig felt the feeling he had felt a few days earlier. A feeling of actually caring about something. It had scared the hell out of him then, and now that he knew the facts, he also knew he was going to have to do something about them.

So, high above the beautiful island of Esmeralda, he flew his Flyin' Machine and tried to sort out the facts. So far, a fellow American, a man named Martin Slate, had floated onto Blackie's Beach and found the masked man, and had also found turtles on the beach. Something that most people had thought was an impossibility.

The news had hit the grapevine via Gorde's wife Vicki, probably because Gorde had talked in his sleep (he'll never learn to keep his mouth shut, even when he's sleeping, Craig thought and chuckled out loud, loud enough that he could hear it over the engine). This news had been bad enough, but when he heard Gorde's friend discovered blue prints for a resort on Blackie's beach Craig's hackles really went up. Enough was enough!

Now, Craig floated above the lagoon, cutting his engine to save gas and letting the natural trade winds blow him softly along the shoreline. Every now and again someone on the beach would wave up to him and he would wave back. He truly loved his little bit of paradise, but he felt as though for the first time in a long time he was going to have to get involved in the ruckus of town, the politics of life. He knew it would be risky to get involved with something of this nature. If his side lost, he would never be able to live on the island in peace again. Even if his side won, he would probably lose his gig at the Hotel Esmeralda, since his employer was Adelante Cortez.

Craig Galetas, sailing through the air, thinking of his part in the rebellion, promptly collided with the side of the mountain, breaking his revelry and nearly breaking his neck. As he gathered up his broken flyin' machine and dragged it back to his palapa, he knew that he was going to be a big part of the meeting at Stan's. He knew he was going to risk it all.

Chapter 17

The sunset, or lack of sunset, troubled many of the older islanders. It was the first time in a long while the setting sun had not entertained them, had not warmed their hearts with a spectacular array of colors, soothed their souls with wispy images gently floating by in the evening sky. This time it hadn't reminded them just how special it was to be a part of this beautiful world of theirs.

Instead, there had been gray, a single, dull, encompassing steel gray that many of the younger islanders had never seen before. But the older folks, who had been around for a long, long time had a lot to say about the sunset, or lack of sunset, just like the one that greeted them the evening before the Taxi Slaughters had broken out.

"Trouble, as big as a marlin, is swimming in our direction," Hector Tranquilleno muttered through a toothless ninety-two year old mouth. Hector, Grandfather of Gorde and son of the great Vicente Ramon Tranquilleno, had seen his fair share of trouble on the island, from the days of the revolution, when Zapata hid on the island, to the modern blood-shed of the Taxi Slaughters. Hector knew trouble when he saw it, and, sure enough, he thought, it was on its way. He could smell it, like rain coming in off the mainland on a stormy winter night.

"Maybe it's a stray low-pressure system off the coast," piped in Gorde's oldest son Armillo, who had been educated on the mainland and knew a fair share about weather.

Hector Tranquilleno, disgusted, stared down his great-grandson and spat, "there's nothing low-pressure about what's going to happen son." And with that, he put his attention back on the gray horizon, took a huge gulp of tequila and sangrita, and hoped above all that this young kid just maybe could be right. That would be a nice surprise, but in his heart of hearts, he had lived on the island too long. He knew what a gray sunset meant.

For many people, those who never really "listened" to the weather, it was no big deal. For Craig Galetas it seemed a little dull, but he hadn't noticed a grayset the last time they had trouble on the island so he wasn't too concerned. He was more worried about how to fix his flying machine.

Chief of police Ramon Ramirez, along with his cousin Mordeno barely noticed the grayset. They were busy playing cards on their deck, and along with the screaming kids, the wind, and the other distractions, they really didn't get a good look at the gray.

Antonio Vargas and his family of fishermen knew one thing, they were not going to go out to sea that evening. It was a ferocious looking storm, gray, thick, dark, and they weren't about to mess with it. These kinds of storms were very rare in the area. So Antonio, knowing he had the night off, had another drink, then another, and slipped into a rare, slightly comatose state of relaxation that he rarely allowed himself.

Vicente Fernandez and Paulo Gabernetti were both frantically driving to each others homes, concerned that another Taxi Slaughter was about to break out. The last time they had seen a gray sky like this was the first night of many deaths. The two old men met on the street, exchanged greetings and slowly, after talking to each other for a few minutes, started to realize they were going to be okay and the clouds weren't particularly directed at them this time. Although they both agreed that there was going to be some big trouble and they had better try to stick together. And then, as they parted, they both yelled out, at the same time, "The Black Sand Resort and Hotel".

Maybe it was just a coincidence, maybe not, but the plotting real estate sleaze, Alfredo Lopez Ramos, having arrived on the late afternoon boat, was at that very minute leaving Adelante Cortez's office after a long and disturbing meeting with the mayor.

Alfredo, although he liked Adelante Cortez and had had a lot of confidence in him, was now losing his patience. Alfredo had always believed that if you wanted something done, you should do it yourself. Still, he couldn't have eradicated the turtles properly, and that's why he had hired the pros, which Alfredo now thought, had really blown the job. Even worse, Adelante had just told Alfredo about the upcoming meeting at Stan's. If a meeting of that sort ever got out to the press, Alfredo knew he was out of business. The Governor would close him down in less than a heartbeat. Alfredo knew that if a resort cost votes, a resort was dead. It was that simple.

So, borrowing a can of gas from his boatman, whom he had hired personally from a place far, far away from the Esmeraldian coast, Alfredo walked directly over to Stan's. Seeing that no one was around, they had all gone off to the shore to watch the sunset, he poured a generous amount of gasoline on the main palapa housing the business. He then set a cigarette down on the far side of the house and walked back to his hotel room like he didn't have a care in the world.

Chapter 18

From the beach you could see the flames from Stan's palapa reaching high up into the sky, turning Esmeralda into one huge united front, ready to do battle against the encroaching powers of greed.

Stan took one look at the flames, realized they were coming from his palapa, turned and took a head count, counting all nineteen family members standing next to him on the seawall, and let out an involuntary long, high squeal of delight while he thought, War! Finally! No more of this piddily tit-for-tat stuff!

Everyone made a run for the flames. Stan, of course, was the slowest of the gang, dragging along his bad leg, cussing at his inability to run with the best of them, and pretty much pissed off that his eighty-one year old body wouldn't perform like his "fifty-one year old mind."

Paulo Gabernetti, the owner of Reliable Taxi, was the first to sputter up to the burning building in his dilapidated 1964 Nova. A typical Reliable taxi, it had shiny bald tires and blue smoke spitting out of the exhaust. The top was whitewashed with the words TAXI in big, bold letters (for God and the birds to see).

Paulo's whole family was piled into his car: his wife Eleni, Paulo Jr., Franco, Helinita, plus two of the family dogs who were barking and yipping and wagging their tails at all the excitement.

Next came Vicente Fernandez dressed in his typical white suit. He drove his spit and polish green and white Volkswagen direct from his sunset celebration. He was still sporting a Pina Colada, complete with pineapple wedge and a little umbrella. He pulled up right next to Paulo and his clan and stuck his head out the window, "Would you look at that! Who would be so stupid?"

Paulo, a little surprised that his archenemy of a million years was so friendly, took a second to realize that with the flames, a new brotherhood was being formed. But he soon jumped in, "Even we wouldn't be so stupid as to do THIS to someone on our island. Ijole brother. What do you think will come of it?"

"I don't know," Vicente said, "but for once in my life, I'm gonna stick around and see."

And then the two men, realizing that they had never really formally introduced each other to their families, gathered together their clans and each one was introduced.

"This is Helinita, she's the third from the last, and she's our swimmer," and "This is Vicente Jr., he's studying French and will be leaving for France in two more years."

Sure, they led different lifestyles, but the underlying reality was they were all islanders, all Esmeraldians and this attack on their turf was sure to bring the whole island, the whole family of Esmeraldians together.

In short order, everyone else in town who didn't have a car showed up, including Magdelina Tranquilleno, who beat the crowd by riding Bromista for the first time in many, many a year. Next to Magda her son, Gorde, came running like a giant elephant being chased by a mouse. Gorde was cussing and spitting drunk, urging his mother to "get off the burro Mama, Por Favor!" His wife Vicki and their whole family followed him.

Craig Galetas excitedly limped in, with Mickey on extra tight reins. Antonio Vargas, fisherman and athlete extradinaire stomped into Stan's yard like a bull ready to do battle, staring at the burned wreckage and saying, "ijole" with a long, smooth, soft but almost guttural tone.

Even Martin, who was fighting a case of turistas again, arrived just steps before Stan. As the flames died down Stan showed up to see the newly formed alliance gathered around in silence.

He checked out the faces in the crowd and saw just about everybody he knew who lived on the island. He knew this would be his moment of glory.

Alfredo Ramos Lopez was conspicuously missing, and, if he were smart, was halfway to the mainland. Adelante Cortez, the minute he saw the flames, had made a run for his office in city hall. He had been frantically trying to call Alfredo, over and over, and each time he dialed, the sound of his tapping fingers reminded him of nails being pounded into a coffin, his coffin. He knew it was just a matter of time.

Henry Ortiz, dumbfounded, upset, disappointed, but not particularly scared for his life (he knew that everybody was aware he was just a pawn and did what he was told—it was his job), stood along the outer fringe of the crowd. He shook his head, saying hello to passersby, knowing that Esmeralda was in for a long night, if they made it through the night.

The meeting began not more than twenty minutes after Alfredo had dropped his cigarette onto the gas. The crowd had all gathered just outside the smoldering remains of Stan's place. Stan, gearing up for the moment, thought this is what it must of felt like to be Knute Rockney, no, General Patton, no, he thought, Eisenhower.

Whatever the case, the half-finished cement "ice cream" storage shed was the only part of Stan's place that survived the brutal torching and now it served as Stan's podium, and natural microphone, broadcasting his message to the crowd.

"Friends, neighbors, Emeraldians..." Stan began, trying to sound important and dignified, "we have reached a point in our village where we must take control of its destiny, we must take a stand...or we will lose our way of life. The devil who lit these fires must be..."

A low rumble stopped Stan in his tracks as Chief of Police Ramon Ramiriz, against his better judgment, but ordered by Adelante, cruised by to check out the meeting. As if given a cue by a Hollywood director of a old fashioned spaghetti western, when Stan stopped talking, over one hundred sets of eyes slowly turned toward the old Dodge Dart, and stared him down so hard he should have turned to stone. But Ramon, averting his eyes, just kept cruising by.

He thought of waving and acting innocent but just before he picked up his arm he caught a glimpse of the eyes—mean, darkly set, then looking for some relief, he turned to the women, only to find they were set a little deeper, a little harder. So he pressed on his gas pedal and told himself he had better ride this one out in his office or even better, in his home.

Stan continued, "The devil who set these fires will have to pay a price. But, I think he was just doing what he was told by his manager, and I think it's time we, as owners of this team, change managers. As the great philosopher Yogi Berra once said…" Stan just stood there, not remembering the quote that he wanted to use. The crowd just stood there too, wondering how they should really react to Stan's sermon and now, to his silence.

Suddenly, the blood in Stan's head, which had been hanging on for dear life for over a minute, drained towards his feet and he felt weak, lost his sense of balance, and his sense of self. Maybe the brisk walk had gotten to him. Nancy, seeing that her ailing husband needed the hook, came out, gently put her arm around him and said softly to the crowd, "Viva la Esmeralda" and got the first round of applause of the meeting.

After she set her husband back in a hammock, where, in reality, he was most effective, where his blood flowed best, she returned to face the crowd. She knew what her husband was trying to say, and she knew what the crowd wanted to hear.

"We are a proud people, and we are a people who have lived together for generations without this kind of trouble. We could have been killed, for what? My children could have been killed."

When she said children her voice quavered and every Mother's spine instantly tingled, hackles went up and suddenly there was an almost audible hum in the audience.

"And so I ask you all, to remain calm, think about how we can find out who is responsible for this and make sure it never happens again. We don't want another Taxi Slaughter, que no. But we also can't let the person who did this walk free. Does anyone else have anything to say?"

After a long silence Craig Galetas, newly inspired and armed and ready with a new determination to take risks, stood up and blurted out, "We all know who is behind this. Where is he. Where is Adelante?"

From the rear Stan raised up his cane and called out, "Let's lynch the Pargo!"

"How do we know he did it?" someone yelled out from the crowd.

"Oh come on. If he didn't do it, it was his idea," Craig stammered.

But Nancy raised up and firmly bellowed, "I don't think he has the huevos for this. I think it was an outside job."

Silence…which meant everyone was in agreement.

Henry, standing not more than ten feet from Craig, couldn't believe his ears. Craig, who was employed by the Hotel Esmeralda, was saying things like this…"ay Chihuahua, we're in for a long night," he whispered. Henry started to back out slowly from the crowd. He could be next, he thought as he bumped into a huge, chubby, yet immovable wall named Gorde.

"Where ya goin' cuz?" Gorde chuckled.

"Oh, I was just…"

But before he could get out his whole sentence his breath was taken away when Gorde abruptly picked Henry up, high above the crowd and said, "Maybe Henry knows who did it? Or at least, where Adelante could be…Henry?"

For a moment Henry thought he should hold out, after all, it was his boss, his livelihood. But then again, this was his life, his livelihood so to speak. Sitting there, high above the crowd, just for a moment, he fantasized that he was the hero, that the whole crowd was looking at him because he had just come back from a war and everyone loved him. Just for a moment, he felt strong, admired and brave. And then he saw their eyes, not the same eyes he had seen over the years across the coffee table. These eyes were worried and serious.

Fearing that he could become the target of their wrath, Henry obliged, "I think he's at home, watching the sunset, or at the hotel. Yes, probably the hotel."

Gorde gently set him down. Henry, who really didn't want to run and warn his boss about the impending doom, figured it really didn't matter if Adelante knew or not. So, he just stood and smiled and waved and was glad that his life had been spared…for now.

Nancy took control of the crowd again.

"Listen up, folks. Listen up. We haven't talked about what really matters here. We must work together to save our turtles. We must work to let Nando live out his final days in peace, as he deserves. And we must work together to save the black sand beach for the turtles."

Everyone was listening, the humm was getting more audible and people were chirping in, saying things like, "Si, es verdad. It's the truth. We must! Viva Esmeralda! Viva las tortugas!"

"If we're not careful we will end up like the mainland slaves…working all day for our food, and nothing else, toiling away at jobs that sap the life right out of our bones, Nancy continued. "It's bad enough what has happened to our island over the last hundred years, but this, if this is allowed to take place, we'll lose everything. Everything that we live for will be gone—the bees, the flowers, the fish. Our children will end up working for other people they don't even know."

Nancy paused to let the last sentence sink in, but she didn't need to. The hackles of the whole village were up, each person like a hair of a dog's back standing straight up, together, to form a strong, unified group of angry hairs, ready to do battle.

The women of the village had started to move gradually to the front of the crowd, and now they comprised the first third of the pack. In front were the oldest, many alive for the Taxi Slaughters. They had in fact been responsible for helping to solve the crisis by going on strike and not using cabs for market day, card day and church day. Now here they stood, old, gray and wrinkled but with eyes full of life.

Gorde's mother Magdelina was part of this pack and, as far as most knew, she hadn't said more than a sentence in the last ten years. But now, she spoke up in a firm if not very loud voice: "We should enforce the law of Emiliano. He knew what was what! Then everybody would get what they need and when the next person came along, they'd get their fair share too."

She was referring to Emiliano Zapata, who lived in the mind of many on the island as the only true law, without order, that was needed. Many of the older folks cheered and yelled, "Viva Zapata," when Magdelina finished and waved to the crowd.

But the younger folks realized they could quote all the Emiliano they wanted but it wasn't going to stop the powers that be from coming in and raping their island. They knew they needed something more. So, after a silence long enough to be respectful, Gorde chirped in, "Maybe that's a good idea. Maybe we should make OUR own land laws so the Pargo and his buddies can't come in and steal our land."

More applause, especially from the under fifty crowd. But then, from the back of the "podium" Stan himself raised up and yelled out, "We don't need laws or government. That's what got us in this god damned mess in the first place."

Nancy, looking right into her husband's eyes replied, "If WE don't make them, somebody else will!"

"The only rule should be no rule," Stan spat back, adding, "I've never seen anything that has rules work."

"There are rules in baseball," Nancy said, and with that the whole crowd started to laugh, with someone yelling out, "Three strikes and you're out Hijo!"

But Stan wasn't about to give up, and standing again, seeing if he could tempt his blood into staying in his head for more than a minute, continued. "It's not about us," he said, as he hugged his wife and looked at his kids. "It's about them," and looking at his gang his eyes began to water, and everyone in the crowd began to look at their kids, and get watery eyed. Stan, knowing that he had finally figured out what he had been angry about for so many years said, "We must unite for our children, so they will have an island here when they grow up, and not an Acapulco."

Craig Galetas, about the only one on the island who didn't have any kids, said, "We need to take care of these good folks, we should rebuild their home…tonight!" With that he went up, hugged Stan and Nancy and proclaimed to the crowd, "I'm going to give them a night at the hotel on…on Adelante. So they have a place to stay while we fix the place up a bit."

With this proclamation the crowd hooped and hollered and joked and said things like, "That would be the day when Stan would even set foot on that Pargo's hotel," or "Yeah, and who would pay for it, the Esmeralda Land Barons," and "Maybe he could take his whole family out to dinner at the hotel's dining room?"

With the last sentence, Stan, not being the kind of guy who could pass up a good opportunity for revenge, said, "Hijos, come on, I'm getting hungry. We're off to the hotel."

Nancy just about fainted, and many in the crowd hooted and hollered and thought he was kidding, but Stan was serious, and he said, "Come on Nance. Gather the kids!"

And amidst a cheering that should have wakened the dead, and could be heard all the way to city hall, Stan and his clan of nineteen set off toward the Esmeralda Hotel.

The crowd slowly dispersed, except Antonio Vargas and a few of his sons, Craig, Gorde and his clan, and believe it or not, even Henry stuck around to help rebuild the palapa.

Meanwhile, still in his office, still deliriously dialing and re-dialing his phone, the mayor of Esmeralda, sweating and now cussing, heard a peculiar sound of cheering. Now in a whole lot of trouble and knowing he had a limited amount of time on this here island, and hopefully not a limited amount of time on this here earth, he waited for the cheering to come closer. Waited for the mob to come crashing down his locked door. He waited like a prisoner looking up at the guillotine about to come flying down on his neck, only he was beginning to notice this guillotine had a very dull blade.

Chapter 19

Adelante Cortez, politician supreme, only took one full day to snap out of his shock. After telling everyone in the village that he had absolutely nothing to do with the burning of Stan's house,(which no one believed, except Stan and his family, who actually were able to keep the truth under wraps for awhile to add to Adelante's pain and suffering) Adelante set out to repair his ruined reputation.

He had to save the resort and get on with business as usual. He had a plan. And if it worked, he could still salvage what was left of his empire. He went to Henry's office to hash over some details and found the door locked, the lights out, with a sign that read, "Closed until further notice" hastily written right on the door.

Ramon Ramirez, chief of police, pulled up, having been summoned by Adelante. "I think Henry's gone AWOL Adelante."

"What do you mean?" questioned the mayor.

"I saw him working on Stan's yesterday. I think he's—"

"Stan's!" the mayor yelled, "What's he doin' that for?"

"I think he wanted to save his skin. When I drove by yesterday, I caught a glimpse of Henry on Gorde's shoulders, with everybody looking at him…I think they twisted his arm…que no."

"Fine. We're meeting in my office with Alfredo," Adelante replied, noticing that when he said the words Alfredo the chief of police winced, looked down to the ground, and when Adelante turned away, Ramon made a small sign of the cross just above his lips. Adelante caught a glimpse of this out of the corner of his eye.

"You suddenly find religion," Adelante emulated Ramon's sign of the cross as they walked toward his door.

"Oh…Well. Adelante. You know Alfredo is a dead man. I really don't even want to sit next to him. You know what I mean." Then, after a few more steps, Ramon added, "You sure it's a good idea to let him back on the island?"

They entered the office and there he sat, the "dead man" in all his gold and silver glory, with a shit-eating grin on his face. "Brilliant idea, Adelante. A brilliant idea. A referendum will certainly save face and if the Fed's ever do find out about what we've been up to, well, we at least can tell them the people were involved, que no?"

As the three men sat down, a sound came from outside the window, "Pissssssstttt. Pissssssttttttt!"

They looked up to see a man with a basket on his head, with a multi-colored cloth covering his face. He was using both hands to keep the basket balanced, and having a hard time of it, when he finally said, "Will you let me in…it's Henry."

Ramon jumped up, opened the door and ushered Henry into the office. Henry, sweating, a little scared and disoriented from the cover, promptly put down the basket, took off the cloth and said, "Adelante. We have trouble. They're talking about hanging you by your…well, your nose. I don't think they are joking this time. I felt it was my duty to tell you. But this is where I get off. Que no. I don't want to go to war with this village. I live here, Que no! So, consider this my resignation." And with that, he put the basket back on his head. Looking both ways to make sure no one was watching, he headed out the door, leaving the mayor, the chief of police and the real estate developer to watch him scurry down the road with the basket on his head.

"What was that?" Alfredo laughed. "Has Henry lost his cookies?"

"No," Ramon grunted, "He's just feeling the wind blowing."

"What does that mean?" Alfredo said, turning to Ramon with narrow eyes.

"The shit is going to hit the fan. I hope you understand that. And you, my friend, are the main turd."

Alfredo got up from his chair, looking at Adelante, then back to Ramon, "Who's side are you on, slimeball?"

Ramon, standing his ground, looked Alfredo right in the eyes, "I'm just stating a fact. That's all."

"Okay, okay, listen guys," Adelante urged, "Let's cut the crap and get down to business here. Please. What's happening on the mainland?"

"Well," Alfredo said, taking a deep breath and then slowly exhaling, "things don't look too great, to be honest."

"Yeah," Ramon said, "tell me something I don't know."

Alfredo continued, ignoring Ramon's comment, "and, of course, Governor Delgado is getting very concerned, Roberto Cristanto and Javiar Garcia Sanchez both met with me this morning and they think they can hold out for awhile before they officially have to pull out of the project."

"So what you're telling me is we're sunk," Adelante nearly cried out.

"No my friend," Alfredo said, "I'm just saying we have to be smart. And your idea to have an election, to dangle the money carrot…that's a good one."

"I don't know," Adelante whined, "I was a little desperate when I thought it up."

Ramon squirmed in his seat. He knew that the people on the island had had enough and no matter what these two politicians schemed up, the cards were dealt and he was holding deuces.

Alfredo turned to them both and started his sales pitch, "Listen to me. We can set up the vote. Make it a big deal. Of course, we'll make sure that we win. And maybe by the time we really get around to breaking ground on the hotel, we'll be able to hire some of these local jamokes, put a few pesos in their pockets, and then they won't want a revolution. I guarantee you that!"

Ramon just shook his head. This guy was definitely from the mainland, and he had no idea who he was dealing with. These were his people. They didn't care about a few pesos, and they weren't gonna be tricked by some stupid vote. Who does he think we are, idiots?

Adelante, reaching for straws, or reaching for a way to get that guillotine away from his neck, started to buy into the idea, "Okay. So we have a vote. We stuff the ballots, otherwise, we won't have any votes to count. And we declare that we won. Great. But we better come through with some jobs for these folks."

"We will, we will," Alfredo assured his partner. And the developer knew he had Adelante. He also knew that he hated the cop's guts and that he would never sit in another meeting with him, because he wasn't buying, and if he was on our side and he wasn't buying, well, Alfredo thought, this might get a little more complicated than he thought.

But within half an hour, Alfredo and Adelante were both convinced that their plan was a hit. Ramon excused himself, saying he had better get back on patrol, since things, "were a little tense in the village," and scooted out of the meeting, trying to wipe the muck off his soul.

And before the day was out, Alfredo and Adelante had set a date for the vote, figured out what their ballot would look like and also decided how to easily insure they had a clear victory. That night they sat in the Hotel Esmeralda's bar, sipping on their champagne, when Ernie, the barkeep, handed Adelante a bill of $1,234 pesos, saying, "Stan said it was on you." When Adelante gave Ernie a double take, Ernie just shrugged, smiled, "What could I say. He had fifty people, I was all alone. You were nowhere to be found."

It was just the bar bill. Within five minutes the hotel Manager came out with the bill for the five rooms which came to an even $5,000 pesos, with a note attached that read, "thank you…Pargo!"

Chapter 20

Emiliano Vargas, the father of Antonio Vargas the fisherman, was a bit of an anomaly even for the people of Esmeralda. No one could remember when he came to the island, although some seemed to think it was around 1915 or so. Since Emiliano had such a different look than the "natives," it was taken for granted that he wasn't born on the island. His broad rimmed sombrero, nearly as old as he was, made him stand out even more. No one else on the island would even think of wearing a hat like that and even if they wanted to, there was no place to purchase one. But for Emiliano the hat had protected him from the elements for years, from the sun especially, when he was out tending to his corn. He still, at the ripe age of God knew what, tended to a small field of corn in the high mountains. So even though Emiliano had raised a whole family of fishermen, he still had a passion for corn because, for Emiliano, corn was life itself.

When asked about his younger years, Emiliano cracked a toothless grin, peered below his ever-present sombrero and mumbled "Ay Chihuahua" or something about Chihuahua. Since many of the folks couldn't really understand a word he said, they took him for face value, an honest, decent, hardworking man who cut a strong edge on your tools and sang some very interesting folk songs. He played his sharpening stone much like a trumpet, able to control the "notes" by the amount of steel on stone. His songs were sad Ranchero songs about lost love, lost land, lost hope and revolution.

As the village pulled together, gathering up their resources much like a country does when in the midst of a war; Emiliano's battle cries struck an emotional cord with the people of Esmeralda. Suddenly, they understood every word Emiliano Vargas sang. And Emiliano Vargas made a killing. It all started when the men from Hermana had come over the hill to help build Stan's palapa. Part of Emiliano's business was sharpening machetes, and he immediately noticed a sharp increase in customers.

So Emiliano, not one to let a good opportunity pass him by, set up shop right behind Stan's special addition (Esmeralda's new symbol of independence) and pumped and sharpened and sang and sharpened. Nestled there under the shade of a huge palm tree, Emiliano, full of adrenaline from his newfound audience, worked away, hoping his legs and lungs could keep up with the growing line of customers. Normally, Emiliano had to haul his semi-portable sharpening unit from location to location, practically begging people to sharpen their tools, machetes and knives. He was part of the early morning chorus, yelling out, "Machetes, knives, tools—sharpened," while he rolled his converted 1964 faded-purple Schwinn stingray, with the back tire swapped out for a huge sharpening stone, around the town, searching for work.

But now, the whole village was lining up to sharpen their machetes. Nancy and the kids were handing out free ice cream to all comers. To Stan, sitting in his hammock and hearing the constant grinding and singing of Emiliano at work, it truly was the sweetest music he could ever imagine. But he wished for the first time in his life, that he lived close enough to the hotel Esmeralda so the Pargo son of a bitch could hear the sound of the coming revolution too.

Emiliano was so busy his legs hurt and he swore that he could actually see the size of his sharpening stone diminishing by the hour. He figured it was because of the massive amounts of new machetes he was getting. To give a new machete a proper edge took up to thirty minutes and a lot of leg power.

The process was simple enough, Emiliano would sit on the long banana seat, peddle the back "tire" which was now a huge sharpening stone that spun around in a slow yet powerful motion, then, gingerly at first, then more boldly, hold the edge of the machete up against the stone. Even though most machetes were sold with an edge, the islanders knew they were pretty much worthless until Emiliano worked them over.

And then, once they had a good, strong edge, they were so sharp you could slice through a coconut like a guillotine through a…Pargo's neck.

Just about the time the whole town was fully armed with razor sharp machetes,(and Emiliano, nearly out of breath, nearly out of leg power, was singing at the top of his lungs to a full house audience) one of Stan's son's looked up to the calendar and realized it was time for the annual "Taxi and Tequila" cockfights. The edges would have to hold because the rebellion of Esmeralda would have to wait…it was party time.

Chapter 21

The 33rd annual "Taxi and Tequila" cock fight was held on a clear, full moon-lit night, the very same day Adelante Cortez announced a vote was going to be held to decide whether the Black Sands Resort should be built on Nando's beach.

And, as always, everyone wanted to attend the event, including Martin Slate, who had been missing from the scene with a bad case of "traveler's diarrhea," which, Martin told anyone who would listen, "nearly killed me!"

In fact, Martin had the honor of traveling to the fights that night with the honored guests, Paulo Gabernetti and Vicente Fernandez.

Unfortunately for Martin, Paulo drove rather erratically. He arrived at Martin's compound with his "new friend" Vicente sitting in the rear seat, skidding through the driveway, coming to a dusty, noisy stop. Martin got in the passenger seat, and immediately felt a sense of doom. He realized his fear of passenger seats, especially this passenger seat, had not faded with the passing of time.

It had all started with the crash a little over three months ago. Martin was in the passenger seat of a red Ford Courier as it blasted sixty miles an hour through the open California desert. When he looked over to his friend who was supposed to be driving, his heavyset buddy was slumped over the driver's wheel, sound asleep—snoring! For a moment, just a fleeting nanosecond, Martin wanted to briskly grab Matt's nose and cut off his air supply—just to see if he'd wake up. But Matt woke up and attempted to guide the speeding truck back onto the pavement.

When the tires gripped the road the truck flipped and slid two hundred yards—upside down in the wet, damp darkness. Martin ended up getting the worst of the injuries with goose egg sized bumps on his head that was sheared off at the top. They waited three hours for help. When help arrived, the retired couple tried to disinfect Martin's head wound with rubbing alcohol.

It sent him into shock. Martin's eyes rolled back in his head and he flipped on the wet pavement like a fish on a sandy shoreline. When he came to, the ambulance driver immediately strapped him onto the stretcher and drove him through the desert at one hundred and ten miles an hour. All Martin could moan was, "Slow down. Please. Slow down!"

"We haven't even left the driveway," Paulo said to Martin, wondering why he was whispering "slow down, slow down". This kid's a nut Paulo thought, "Can we go now?" he said.

"Sure," Martin said, snapping out of his revelry and taking a good look at Paulo's car.

Paulo, not one to worry much about the condition of his Taxis, worried even less about the condition of his own car, which was a VW Thing. Vintage 1977, orange—or what used to be orange—and, as Martin was finding out this very minute as they drove through the dark night, needed a new front end, BADLY!

Paulo's car swerved to the right, then to the left and Martin, who had had his share of auto accidents this past year, yelled, "Jesus Christ Paulo! Could you keep your eyes on the road!"

"They're on the road," the veteran Taxi driver calmly said, pretty much used to his fares yelling and screaming and begging for their life before they were politely dropped off at their destination.

"What the hells the matter with this car?" Martin begged, as they passed one of the few lights in town and he saw that Paulo was in fact driving a straight line, it was just the car (swiveling and bumping along the dirt road) that couldn't go straight.

"I imagine having a front end would help," Vicente chirped in, with a wide grin, then added, "but hey, we're moving along at a pretty good clip here, huh friend," he said, patting his new buddy Paulo on the shoulder, "What more could you ask for?"

"A bathroom," Martin said, only half-joking.

Martin couldn't believe he had put himself in this position. He popped a few more Peptos into his mouth as they turned out onto the main highway, which was paved, and he just knew he wasn't going to hold out. They didn't know he'd had two back-to-back car accidents; one splitting open his head and leaving him with little pieces of stone to this very day coming out of his head, the other a week later when his buddy Scott had lost his brakes and nearly murdered him.

The one thing they knew was they had a very antsy passenger.

"Calm down Hijo. We're almost there," Paulo said, smiling at Martin and giving him a reassuring nod. It was something Paulo would have never done years ago. But he had mellowed with age and this young kid, well, his veins were starting to pop out of his head.

Then Vicente, tossing a small crumpled roll of toilet paper forward to Martin, gaily added: "If you need to go, we can pull over. I used to drive all over town looking for a clean bathroom. I wasn't going to stop until I found one. Well, my friend, unless you're out in the boonies at Craig Galetas's place, there just isn't one."

This kind of frankness was new for Vicente too. He never talked like this with his family and he really didn't have any friends. But today, somehow, he felt free. This was fun. He sat back, let the wind blow through his hair and thought about some of the mistakes he'd made over the years. How he could have been a little looser in his younger years, and now, how he should really try to enjoy every minute of what was left of his life.

The two taxicab company owners truly had changed a lot over the years. Now in their mid-seventies, life had dealt them their fair share of deuces. Paulo Gabernetti wasn't going to be saving lives by giving anybody a drop kick at tonight's event because in the last year he had suffered four heart attacks. The last one should have been it, but much to Paulo's chagrin at the time, Vicente had repaid the favor of many years back and saved his life. So now things were even and they could be friends, because Vicente no longer owed him a life.

It had been quite heroic too. Early one morning Paulo was out walking the shallows of the fisherman's beach. He loved being in the water, just so he didn't have to get into a boat. Not many people were around, but Vicente just happened to be passing by, walking his dog—at the right place, at the right time.

Paulo, grabbing his chest in pain, was struggling for the shore when he fell in the shallow water. In fact, he was about to drown when Vicente, running through the soft, thick sand with everything he had, dashed down to the shore and pulled Paulo from the soup.

Paulo's lips and face were blue. His pulse faint. So Vicente, cussing and telling his longtime enemy/friend/saver of his life that if he didn't pull out of it, he was going to kill him and started to pound on his chest.

"Come on, you old son of a bitch," he yelled as he pressed, "come on!"

Nothing. Vicente didn't quite know what to do, but he had seen it in the movies, read about it some fifty years ago, and, it looked like he had nothing to lose, so he gave Paulo mouth to mouth. But Paulo, being his cantankerous self, even in his moment of death, wasn't going to come to. Vicente blew into his mouth, pinched his nose, did everything he could to save his counterpart. And Paulo, in what could have been his final insult to his rival, threw up all over Vicente.

"Ahhhhhhh," Vicente moaned, wiping the barf off his face and pants. "Well then," he screamed, turning to leave, "die you son of a bitch."

He took a few steps and then for good measure gave Paulo one last swift kick in the chest.

Paulo promptly came too, looked up at Vicente and said, "What?"

"I just saved your worthless life. I don't owe you anything," Vicente yelled. "Nothing!"

"How do I know you saved my life?"

Vicente looked around for witnesses. None. Oh boy, he thought, this old son of a bitch isn't gonna give it to me. So there they were, frozen in time, both with rather dumbfounded looks on their faces, not knowing how to solve a rather uncomfortable situation.

It took a few minutes for Paulo to catch his breath and during that time he noticed the barf all over his cohorts' chest and the pained expression in his face. Much to Vicente's surprise, Paulo motioned for Vicente to help him up and said softy, "gracias."

So, without really saying it, without making a big issue out of it, without doing the usual island watusi, Paulo and Vicente were even. Paulo wasn't even sure why he had said thanks. Maybe he was tired of the battles, he thought. After seventy years of battling, why not just let someone win one?

Still, as Paulo joked a few days after the incident, in front of Vicente and a large group of people, "If you wanted to kiss me, why didn't you just say so?"

Vicente Fernandez had spent the last thirty-three years trying to get his family to understand why he had agreed to this unorthodox tradition of cock fighting for taxi territories. The day his father and grandfather had found out about the arrangement Vicente had been banished from the family.

Plain and simple, to them, it was a barbaric arrangement. They didn't want any part of, and they were embarrassed and ashamed that one of their offspring would even consider such an event. It was not the way to do business.

Vicente's reaction to all this was to get extremely ill with an ear infection and lose eighty percent of his hearing. Still, Vicente, who used to be a family man, doing and saying what ever his father and grandfather thought correct, had felt suddenly free. Sure, he drowned his sorrows in a daily chocolate sundae. Vicente, once tall, proud, lean, had put on about eighty pounds and now sported a pot-belly that he showed off like a prize winning watermelon by unbuttoning the bottom three buttons of his shirt. Besides his loss of hearing and his weight, he thought, it had turned out to be a good thing.

So now, finishing up what for Martin was one of the longest car rides of his life, Martin, Paulo and Vicente plowed up to the arena, a small area that had been fenced off in front of someone's country home. An old parachute top had been suspended into the air to make a cover. Two and a half foot high plywood, in a circle about thirty feet across, made up the ring.

The trio was the last to arrive and just about all two hundred seats that circled the arena, some on the floor, others grandstand style, were taken. Two ringside seats, one on the side painted red, the other on the green, were set aside for the owners.

Of course, the dirt had been carefully manicured in the traditional way, with colored waters and flowers. Inside the arena two distinct roosters had been drawn in the dirt, complete with red and green coloring. Along with ice cream, Stan and Nancy were serving food. Gorde Tranquilleno and his wife Vicki served up beer, wine, tequila and sangrita (they had made a pretty penny off this crowd already!).

The red side was the local island handler, Antonio Vargas. Antonio, when he was not fishing or competing in a triathlon, raised fighters and he had a pretty good record. The green side was the visitors from the mainland—from Tuxla Guiterrez, Southern Mexico, known for their own rebellions and good fighting birds.

Both Vicente and Paulo hoped to get the green visitors side, because they looked strong.

After the flip of the coin there would be seven fights before the main event, the fight that would determine who got to pick which side of town they could have for their territory.

The announcer introduced the owners and they entered the ring, Paulo dragging his bad leg and Vicente, patting his belly and waving to the crowd. The crowd went wild. It had officially begun. This was Paulo's year to toss the coin. The announcer built up the tension by reminding everyone what was at stake. He told of all the territories that would be chosen by the winner, the millions of pesos that would change hands (which everyone knew was an exaggeration by millions). He really made it sound like the world depended on who won. And of course, the whole crowd went along with the announcer, believing that everything did depend on the final fight.

Gorde's line suddenly got longer. People were ordering double, triple, even quadruple margaritas. Or just purchasing a bottle each of Gorde's tequila, sangrita, and grabbing from the big box full of limes. The announcer went on and on, and finally, after a ten-minute monologue he asked for the coin. Out came a wooden box, inside the red and green coin lay on deep purple felt.

Paulo picked the coin up, showed both sides of it to the crowd and then threw the coin high in the air. It landed in the soft, raked dirt right in the middle of the arena—red. Paulo didn't show it, but he was a bit disappointed. But who knows, he thought, maybe this year Antonio could have a real fighter. His father Emiliano was certainly on a roll, and he would be sharpening the curved pieces of metal that would be attached to Antonio's fighters.

In the green seats, which were the visitors seats and the cheap seats sat; Gorde's whole family, including his mom Magdelena, Stan and Nancy's whole troop of nineteen and Craig Galetas, who left Mickey behind. Henry and his wife Gabriela were chumming with Stan's kids, even though Henry every now and again would look over to his ex-boss Adelante and wonder what he had done, how he would survive and what he would do for money.

Adelante Cortez and his wife Gloria sat ringside right in the middle of the red side. Next to him wearing a white shirt stained with beer, was

Alfredo Lopez Ramos. On the other side of Alfredo was the chief of police, Ramon Ramirez, and his whole family. Ramon was trying to distance himself from Adelante and Alfredo by not looking their way very often and not buying them beers.

He knew that although the festival was one of the few times when mortal enemies could sit this close together without a gun going off; he also realized tensions were running high on the island, there were no guarantees.

The event always started out with five or six jesters coming out into the center of the ring, dressed in palm frond shirts and cloth masks—dancing like there was no tomorrow. The deafening music helped keep them energized for their half-hour dance. As the warm-up wound down the music became softer and the announcer pulled out an old deck of playing cards. It was time for Pick-A-Card—a game of luck.

The dancers took off their masks and then got down to business. The head dancer dealt two cards onto the ground about ten feet apart, then threw a third card in the middle, dealing the last one from the bottom of the deck with a flourish. The announcer called out the numbers or faces—"three, eight, king." All the ringmen now worked their section of the ring, trying to get people worked up to bet on their cards. "Three, eight, king" they yelled.

And the money flowed, almost as hard as the tequila. Old men, children and women—everyone from the village put huge amounts of money on their card by handing it to the ringmen. Which card would be the next one on the deck? Which card of the three?

After the announcer realized they had sucked all the action they could from the crowd, he yelled, "Juego." The games began.

All the ringmen immediately stopped taking bets and returned to the center of the ring. The head ringman pulled out the deck of cards. All was still. The music stopped.

Gorde, now ringside, couldn't even breathe. He had put so much money out, so fast, his head spun. Adelante stood up, blocking the view of those behind him. No one said a word. Even the wind that had been a fairly strong breeze, paid homage to the first turn of the card, and with still air, close to two hundred people holding their breath, the first card was turned.

"Seven. Nine. Two".

With each turn of the cards, the crowd took a small breath, then held it again as the ringman paused, then called out the next number, trying to squeeze every last ounce of drama out of the event.

"Four." Then finally, a king softly floated to the ground.

"King," yelled the announcer and the mad scramble began. The ringmen, with fists full of money, went out to pay the people who had bet on the king. How the ringmen remembered who had given how much money was one of the miracles of the event. Rolls of money flew from their pockets, even bigger rolls began to fill the kitty, a brown burlap bag that the announcer kept tied around his waist.

Martin, his first time at a cockfight, watched with wide-eyed fascination. This was the same village where people barely had enough money to scrape together two pesos, he thought. These people are mad.

Martin took a good look around. He took a few more Pepto Bismols. He was feeling worse, but he wanted to see what would happen next. Men, women, children, folks in their nineties, to a person, bombed, smiling, throwing months worth of money into the middle of a finely manicured ring like it was monopoly money.

For the village, the fun had just begun.

For three hours the money and the booze flowed. For three hours, the village was in unison, breathing together, moaning when their cards didn't come up, cheering when they did. Barrels of tequila, gallons of ice cream, enough tamales to feed the twenty million inhabitants of Mexico City were consumed. And the cocks still hadn't come out yet.

Martin sat in awe. The village was treating this like the Olympics, except they were trying to win the award for most beer, tequila and food consumed in a three-hour period. I wonder if they have a medal for that, Martin thought. He heard some people as they came in behind him, one of them bumped his arm with something hard. He turned to see what it was. Five guys with submachine guns stood, watching the event, stone faced. They wore farm worker clothes. He didn't recognize them.

Martin uneasily looked around for Ramon Ramirez and saw him way across the arena in line for a beer. But only five seats down was Mordeno Ramirez. He'll have to do, Martin thought.

He got up, walked over and asked Mordeno not to stare at the five guys over where his seat was. Of course, Mordeno stared right at them, told Martin that he'd never seen them before, then looked back to the ring.

"Usually," Mordeno explained, "we hire some Federales to guard the money. Cause…there's a lot of money blowin' in the wind tonight Martin. But those boys, they don't look like Federales to me. They look like trouble."

The crowd stood up and let out a huge roar. Martin saw that the handlers had arrived and scrambled back to his seat as they entered the ring with their box of magic tricks. The visiting handler was heavy-set with a square jaw, short black curly hair and a big thick black mustache. He was squared off with the villages' very own Antonio Vargas.

The two men came to the middle of the arena while the announcer introduced them and thanked the visitor for honoring the island by coming from so very far away. The men stared at each other and tried to look as mean and aggressive as possible. And the mind games began.

The first roosters came out and were weighed in. Next the metal claws were brought out to the judge, measured to make sure they were equal and then, back in their perspective sides, the handlers wrapped on the claw. The very act of wrapping the claw was an art in itself. There were various techniques, some handlers preferred to put the blade facing the front, some facing the rear. Whatever the angle, it was then attached to the bird's leg using about fifteen yards of fine, strong line.

So Antonio Vargas, from the school of facing forward blades, carried out his piece of metal on a cloth. He did this partly for show and partly because his father was on a roll and had sharpened the blade so precisely he was afraid if he touched it he would surely start spurting blood.

He attached it to the leg of his first bird and with a winding flurry, wrapping all fifteen yards of the purple line around the bird's leg. The blade was now a part of the bird and when he scratched at his opponent, it would be deadly.

Emiliano, still a little sore from all the sharpening he had done in the last forty-eight hours, waited with a sparring bird and when his son was ready, they warmed up the first bird with a little spar. Sure enough, the fighter just barely touched the warm-up bird and it was cut.

"Bastante," Antonio yelled, "Enough."

He didn't want to tire out his bird and the claw seemed to be working perfectly. He didn't want to risk bending it on a piece of a spar bird bone.

Antonio signaled to the announcer that he was ready. The visiting handler, with his huge, twitching mustache did the same. And the crowd's roar went up another notch. Both handlers cleaned their bird's metal claw with lemon and a piece of napkin to prevent infection, because many times, a bird would get wounded, then kill its opponent.

A winning bird, a bird that had the knack of surviving the first thirty seconds of the fight, was a valuable item. Losing it to an infection was always a danger.

The announcer came to the center of the ring, and with a movement of his hand, the music, the hubbub, the world stopped. All was silent. He motioned for the handlers to come center ring.

"Please."

Antonio and the mustache man approached both gently stroking their birds. When they came within two feet of each other they stopped and held out their bird's leg with the metal claw.

"Good," the announcer said checking Antonio's. "Okay," the other. "Juego. Play!"

The announcer backed away. The two handlers, never taking their eyes off of each other, moved back to their sides of the ring. The visitor with the big mustache moved over to a bottle of Chivas Regal, took a long swig, and keeping it in his mouth, suddenly turned his bird around, blew a fine mist of Chivas into the bird's eyes. He turned the bird around again, blew a fine mist into the bird's tail end, then walked in, put his bird down on the ground, ready to fight.

Meanwhile, Antonio, not taking his eyes off the mustache man, took his bird's head, sucked it into his mouth and with a squawk, spit it out, rustled his bird's feathers to make it look bigger and came back into the center of the ring, ready to fight.

Both handlers now backed off, their birds facing each other. The roosters, a little shaken up from all the sucking and blowing and boozing, finally came to and within ten seconds, the fight began. At first, they just pecked, and then all of Emiliano's sharpening paid off in one quick second. Antonio's bird made a move to scratch the opposing bird and with a slash, cut the other bird's throat.

At first blood the crowd roared their approval, getting the birds even more excited.

Not realizing the extent of his damage, the opposing bird tried to retaliate, but soon, whimpering in pain, blood squirting out of the fatal wound, the bird started to run around the arena. Antonio's bird, in hot pursuit, pecked at the wound, opening up the vein and within two minutes, it was over. Antonio had won his first match rather easily. The crowd was now exhilarated, now greedy, now wishing they had bet more money, or wishing they had bet on Antonio's bird. They counted their winnings, their losings, their should have beens, and got ready for the next fight.

Every half-hour, into the wee hours of the morning, new birds would be introduced, the blades would be cleansed with the lemon and the crowd, now quiet, would roar on the first blood. Some of the fights were quick like the first one, others lasted for ten, sometimes fifteen minutes, with knock down, drag out battles.

It was about 4:30 a.m., around the sixth fight, when Martin realized he was ready to leave. He knew the guys weren't leaving and he had found out that the taxis weren't even running tonight because all the drivers were busy losing a month's worth of wages on each fight. So, with the plan of walking back, he stood up to go.

All the music stopped and everyone, to a person, stared right at Martin. Had they somehow figured out he wanted to leave? What was up? It was too soon for the next fight. He turned to ask the person to his right and that's when he saw all five of the gunmen, slowly walking out of the arena, right behind him, with their guns pointed straight up.

Ramon Ramirez was following them out, with his pistol pulled, yelling, "I don't care. I don't care. You can not bring those guns into this arena."

The gunmen waved their guns. Angry. Yelling. The crowd was frozen. Terror. Not a blink. Of the two hundred plus people watching as the gun men turned and yelled back at Ramon, only Martin was stupid enough to look in the direction of the gunmen. One of them made eye contact with Martin and gave him a slight grin and waved his gun toward him. Martin searched for an escape route under the grandstand. He thought this would be a pretty ironic way to go, after his car crashes, to get shot in the head during a cockfight.

The five gunmen stopped and turned on Ramon. "We need to protect our money," was what Martin thought he heard them say…But they were yelling, talking fast and all Martin knew was it didn't look good and at any moment, bullets could fly.

Ramon kept talking, stalling and Martin wondered why he just didn't tell them to get out. Get outside the wire fence. Go!

Then, as quickly as it had started, it ended. All of a sudden all five gunmen's eyes bugged out, they stood up straight, dropped their rifles and, even though Martin and most of the people from his side of the arena couldn't see it, they knew that somebody had them by the proverbial cajones. Five freshly sharpened machetes had pierced the gunmen's shirts and holding onto the other end of these more than razor sharp instruments of destruction were the experienced hands of Emiliano and four other distinguished gentlemen who in no uncertain terms meant business.

"We will help you protect your money," Emiliano gently whispered as he came around to the front side of the gunmen and greeted them with his broad smile and floppy sombrero.

"Gracias," blurted out the one with the red bandana and missing front tooth.

Emiliano looked at the four other men and they all nodded their heads, agreeing it was a very good idea. The guns were laid down on the ground and the men stepped back into the arena area to watch the next fight.

With that, the music came back and the lines at Gorde's bar became the longest of the evening. Martin, thinking that maybe he should stay, popped some more Peptos and settled back into his seat.

Besides, he said to himself, the next one is the deciding fight. How can I leave now?

So, with the horizon turning orange with the first moments of sunrise, the last fight, the battle for the taxi territories, the match all two-hundred and eleven people had been waiting to see for over eight hours, was about to begin. But first, everyone wanted to eat.

During all the gun toting, Nancy, Vicki and about eight other women had been working steadily away on the breakfast—tamales with mole sauce, fresh bread, chicken in mole sauce, tortillas, rice and beans. They jokingly figured there would be a few survivors from the gun battle and they'd probably be hungry.

And now, they served up a feast. And for approximately one hour, the village of Esmeralda was silent, no music, no guns, just the sound of chewing and laughter. By the time the morning chorus of burros, birds, geckos and roosters was over, the crowd was ready for the main event.

Both Antonio and the visitor on the green side had saved their best birds for the final fight. They tied on the claws, wiped them with lemon and warmed up their birds. The green bird was a tall, yellowish bird that seemed full of energy. Antonio had chosen a stocky black bird with huge eyes and short, powerful legs.

The birds were placed in the center and the fight began. Antonio's bird stood still, while the visitor's bird ran around in circles, looking for an opening.

And for close to five minutes they bobbed and ducked, like a boxer and a straightaway puncher, waiting for the other to make a mistake. But both birds, and both handlers had plenty of patience.

The audience, on the other hand, had just about lost theirs. They came for a fight, not a dance. And they started to let the handlers know this: "How 'bout a fight!" "Pollo. Chicken. Where are the roosters?" "Pluck em and eat em."

So the announcer called the first round over without even a peck on the cheek. And the crowd continued to yell. The announcer called the two handlers into the center of the ring, while their assistant held their birds.

"We will have to pluck them," the announcer sternly said, "If we don't get a fight out of them soon."

"Our birds have different styles, que no," the visitor said matter of factly.

Nodding his head in agreement, Antonio said, "I could make my bird angry by plucking a few feathers...that should make him more aggressive."

The visitor agreed, saying, "I will pluck the same amount that you do, in all fairness."

So they returned to their corners, yanked three feathers each out of their birds, and when they squared them off, it was a whole new ballgame. The birds came out angry, went right after each other and pecked and clawed and pecked for ten minutes straight. The crowd went wild. The handlers, proud that their birds were putting on a good show, sat in their corners glowing. It really was a good fight, they thought, even though each of them truly wanted to win, they also liked the act of a good fight.

The tall yellow bird ran in circles, slashing at Antonio's bulky black bird. The bulky black bird, now charging rather than holding its ground, simply ran right into the yellow bird, knocking him over and pecking at his neck.

Neither of the birds used their claws very much and this was what allowed them to fight for so long. When the metal claws came out, the party was usually over—fast.

But this time, after a full fifteen minutes, the claws came out and each bird went for the jugular and each bird was successful in cutting its opponent.

Both birds, completely exhausted, gave their last bit of battle and when it was apparent that even though they were cut, neither of the birds was going to win, at this moment, the announcer called for a break.

Each handler brought their birds to their corners, and as the crowd yelled out encouraging words, they tended to their birds; putting their fingers in the holes to stop the bleeding, re-wrapping their claws, petting them, blowing water or Chivas Regal into their faces and talking to them.

Round three began with a flurry, then slowly, both birds began to run out of gas and finally, when they could barely walk anymore, the judge called time and drew three lines, about a foot apart, and yelled out the word for fifteen, "Quince."

One bird was placed on the outside line, another on the other outside line. The first bird to cross the middle line and stay across for fifteen seconds, while still on its feet, was the winner.

But these birds didn't even want to move. They looked like a couple of punch-drunk boxers, with their heads weaving and bobbling.

Finally, the handlers were allowed to "coax" their birds into moving. The huge mustache from Tuxla-Guiterrez took a giant mouthful of Chivas and blew it right up his bird's butt.

With a squawk and bugged-out eyes, his bird took on a new life. Antonio talked to his bird, and finally in the end, put his birds bloody head into his mouth and spat it out, with about the same effect as the visitor—his bird came back to life.

Both birds were put back on their sides of the middle line, and both birds came out fighting, crossing the middle line, pecking, and then, they sat down, face to face, and bled all over each other. The announcer asked the handlers to put them back on their lines, which they did, and this time, only Antonio's bird crossed the line. And there he was, standing tall and strong and the announcer started to count up to fifteen.

The crowd was on its feet. Their moment of victory. But at the count of fourteen the bird's head hit the ground. Disqualified. But…the announcer hadn't seen this and he proclaimed a victory for Antonio. And while his back was turned, Antonio ran down, blew some air into his birds mouth, reviving him just in time for the announcer to turn around and see an alert, squatty black bird—the obvious winner.

The visitors, and everyone else for that matter, knew the truth. Antonio really hadn't won. The visitors and, for that matter, anyone else who bet on green, were screaming at the top of their lungs.

"No! No! His head dropped. It's not a win. No!"

The announcer said, "What?" pointing to the black bird, that was still standing, while the yellow visiting bird was lying on its side, nearly dead.

Martin was glad the guns had been confiscated. But what's this? The five men, who had come to protect their money, were shooting into the air…with pistols. Where did they get the pistols?

Again, everyone froze. The music stopped. And the leader of the five men jumped over the divider and faced the crowd.

"The red bird's head didn't make a count of fifteen. We need another quince."

The announcer, sweating, a little nervous, said, "sure."

What else could he say. So he lined up the birds for another quince and the visiting bird, although he snapped to for a minute, couldn't even walk. The black bird, thinking that he was the winner, acted like one, crossed the line, pecked a few weak pecks at the visiting bird, and after a slow yet firm count of fifteen, the announcer pronounced the home bird the winner. He turned to the visitor with the pistol and said, "Sorry my friend. I think that's Juego. Game."

The visitors had to admit, it was a fair victory.

They promptly put away their guns, (which made Martin a whole lot happier) ate some tamales and joined the ranks of the other visitors. The visitors, who, at this very moment, seemed to have forgotten that they had lost, were trying to kill off the final gallon or two of tequila before the sun actually came up over the horizon.

So, this year it would be Paulo Gabernetti's choice. And coming to the center of the ring, he announced with the microphone, looking right into his new friend Vicente Hernandez's eyes that he wanted to keep the same territories that he had last year.

When Vicente gave him a quizzical look, Paulo replied with, "I'm too old for change. And I don't want to go to the airport anymore, and, I really don't think most of my cars will make it that far anyway."

With that, Vicente, Paulo and their families finished off the 33rd annual "Taxi and Tequila" fiesta with a small picnic under the shade of the huge Tabacin tree.

Adelante, drunk and feeling like he really was on top of the world, since he had bet big on Antonio's bird, was the first to leave for home. And moments after his car pulled out, Craig Galetas took the microphone from the announcer and slurred, "I want…I want you all to come…to come out to vote today."

The first knee-jerk reaction from the leaving crowd was boos and throwing empty beer cans at Craig, but he continued, "If he wants…if he wants to play the game…we can too. If everybody votes down his Black Sands Resort…thing, whatever the hell it's called. Then what's he gonna do?"

"I second the motion," slurred Stan, "let's slay that Pargo at the polls!" Stan was way back in the kitchen area, where he was helping to load up the ice cream stand. And suddenly, the crowd changed its attitude. Suddenly, it made sense and amidst hoots and hollers, they all slowly left the arena and walked down towards city hall.

About an hour later a very unsuspecting Alfredo Lopez Ramos, who was manning the polls that he had been guaranteed would be empty, sat in disbelief as the whole village voted down the initiative, marking their X's on the ballots. When he ran out of ballots, (they only had twenty) everyone demanded that they mark their X's on a piece of paper.

Two hours and seven hundred and eighty-nine votes later the initiative stood at seven hundred and eighty-nine to one. Adelante showed up, making it an even two. And even Adelante, veteran politician that he was, wasn't quite sure what to do now.

Chapter 22

Adelante Cortez, forever the politician, forever the competitor, and at the moment just a little desperate, wasn't about to give up on his dream. He had finally figured out how to turn around the insult of getting voted down seven hundred and eighty-nine to two. He knew that if he claimed victory the whole village would realize he had stuffed the ballots. But, he surmised, why not just fix the initiative? It was that simple. He'd change a word or two in the ballot so the seven hundred and eighty-nine votes were against NOT building the Black Sands Resort.

And now, satisfied that he had come up with such an original idea (who would really know, the villagers rarely talked outside of their families), his hope was they'd think the other families had voted for the resort, succumbing to the promise of jobs and money and tourists. The only real problem, was how to break this wonderful news to the town folk.

So, with this idea firmly in hand, Adelante walked into his own hotel, into his own bar, which at three o'clock in the afternoon, was empty, and proceeded to get stinking drunk. Why? Well, he still hadn't come up with plan on HOW to break the news. And, knowing the town, it was going to be a risky proposition.

So he drank his rum and cokes, and pondered, hoping an answer would arrive from the ethers. When it didn't he stumbled over to Lola's for a haircut, thinking maybe the act of getting his haircut would jar something loose.

Lola's House of Beauty, not more than half a mile from the hotel, on the lagoon side of town, truly was situated in Lola's house. In fact, her living room faced the lagoon and the soft chatter of sea gulls. Lola, in her mid-forties, was a mother of four kids, had three cats and a house that looked like it had never been cleaned, although every Sunday she gathered up the kids, scared away the cats, and put the place sort of back together, to start the week fresh.

Her home was really just a big living room that hadn't been quite finished. Her second husband had promised to finish it, but he had promised a lot of things and had only given her two more mouths to feed.

The floor, although it was dirt, had been carefully polished and watered and tramped down in the traditional way, so it looked more like a dark, finely polished wood and acted the same. When she cut hair, she could sweep it off the floor, and to a hair, it would all come up in her dustpan, without disturbing the hard packed surface.

Lola's haircuts were the most expensive in town. Many of the elite, including the Chief of Police, the few wealthy retirees and of course, Adelante, came to Lola's on a regular basis. Others came for special occasions, like a wedding or a funeral. Because, after all, she was the only person on the island who had actually gone to beauty school on the mainland. Even so, her regulars had the tell-tail signs of being a customer of Lola—scars behind their ears. It wasn't that Lola didn't know what she was doing, because she truly did give a good cut. It was just...her kids.

And right now, as Adelante sat in the chair, his ears and neck covered with shaving cream for the final razor clean up. Lola used a single-edged razor held between her thumb and index finger. The kids came roaring through the living room door arriving home from school, totally oblivious to their mom and her customer, as if she had never had a customer in their living room, ever!

Racing through the house hoping for hot corn tortillas in the kitchen, Roberto, the nine-year-old, bumped Lola's hand just a she pressed it firmly behind Adelante's ear.

"Owwwwwwwhhhllllll," Shrieked the mayor, then, "Shit. That was deep!"

"Roberto! Roberto, you little good for nothing…" and then, Lola, turning to Adelante, "I'm sorry my friend."

She leaned over, purposely placed her cleavage right in the Mayor's face and kissed his bloody ear, right next to the fifteen or so other scars.

"Oh," moaned Adelante, "Oh…I think I'll live."

Lola, like many barbers around the world, had a special connection with her clientele and in a strange yet wonderful way, after she nicked them, and kissed them on the ear, they normally revealed their inner most secrets to her. And Lola, being the professional that she was, never, ever "spilled the beans." And that's why, when Adelante caught his breath after this ever so long kiss on the neck, he started to tell Lola all about his plan to ensure his future years of wealth.

As he let it fly, Lola's eldest son, Eduardo, sat in the kitchen, eating corn tortillas. Eduardo just happened to be friends with Stan's son Rico, and the Mayor, a bit drunk and way too loud, proudly yelled to Lola, "We're going to fix the vote on the Black Sands Beach so I'm gonna win and when I do, I'm gonna be rich."

"That's good my friend. Keep it down," urged Lola.

But the Mayor didn't hear a word she said, and continued his tirade, "And when I'm rich, I'm gonna back you, so you can have a fancy salon to service all the tourists, right there in the resort. Won't that be great!"

"Thank you Adelante" Lola cooed, thinking it was nice he said that, but four or five of her customers had already told her that the whole town had voted against the initiative.

"I heard that maybe it was a close vote, que no?"

The Mayor, not wanting to ruin his dream, spilled the big beans, and spilled them loud and clear, so even if Eduardo weren't listening, which he was, he still would have heard.

"Not so, well, we made a few adjustments. We kinda fixed things. And we're gonna win by a landslide. You just wait and see! We're not sure how we're going to make the announcement. But it will come soon."

Not soon enough for Adelante. He never even made it out of the chair when five masked men, wearing full-faced black ski masks, entered the front door. And what a sight these masked men were. They looked kind of familiar to Adelante, and really familiar to Lola, but what was she gonna say. She lived in the village and she knew what side her tortilla was toasted on.

The tall, skinny one with the white skin, who was now checking the window, then nervously looking around the room, nearly jumped right out of his mask when one of the other men stomped his foot.

The biggest man, weighing in at least two hundred and fifty pounds, two fifty-eight to be exact, huffed and puffed and stunk of tequila. Yet he moved with the grace of a ballerina, right over to the Mayor who still sat with shaving cream all over his neck. As the big man slowly put the dull side of a machete against the Mayor's throat, he softly asked in a badly disguised voice, "Would you like a shave?"

The Mayor, thankful this huge man with the familiar breath, (a mix of sangrita and tequila thought the Mayor) didn't use the sharp side of the machete, quickly joked back, "No thank you, I've already been nicked today."

Which got a roaring round of laughter from the crowd of five and Lola. They laughed so hard it took them a full minute to settle back down to business. Adelante laughed too. But even though he was drunk, his laughter came out a bit tight and nervous.

"What can I do for you gentlemen?" Adelante asked, trying to keep his cool. Knowing that if he panicked they would slice him into ribbons right there and feed him to the sharks for dinner.

Another masked man, who kept trying to tuck his long blond hair back into his cap, had the distinctive knotty knees of an old-time surfer who had learned to surf back when you paddled on your knees. He blurted out, "We hear the results of the vote are official. And we'd like to hear who won."

"Well," Adelante stalled, "we haven't officially counted the ballots yet."

Suddenly, another masked bandito, dragging one bad leg painfully along, cussing at this very same leg every step of the way, moved over near the mayor and placed his machete, with the sharp side forward, right under the mayor's hooked nose.

The mayor held his breath while the masked man muttered, in the oldest voice of the five: "Your day has come. You Pargo son-of-a-bitch. We're going to string you up and pour honey all over your body and feed you to the bees. If they'd eat you."

The final masked man, a little smaller than the rest, and with a higher, younger voice, even though it was disguised the best he could do, said, "Dad, come on, we can't really DO THAT, can we?"

"Don't call me that," the older man yelled, pulling the machete away from the Mayor and turning nervously to the rest of them, saying, "Do you believe this kid. You'd think he was somebody else's." And turning to the kid, "Didn't I teach you better?"

The other three masked men got a great laugh out of "Dad", who had pretty much admitted now that this kid was his son. Lola thought if the Mayor needed any other clues, they could also give him their addresses and phone numbers.

Of course, the Mayor had stopped trying to figure out who these masked men were when he felt the cold sharp edge of a freshly sharpened machete, and started trying to figure out how he was going to get out of this jam—alive.

While the kid sheepishly held his head down, the "Dad" turned his attention back to the Mayor, again putting the blade right under the man's hooked nose.

"We really DON'T want to hurt you. But we're not going to stand for this resort, que no?"

All the other masked men nodded their heads, with the kid nodding really hard, like it was going to make up for his blunder of calling his father Dad in front of the mayor, God and the universe.

The tall masked man with the white skin kept checking the windows, peeking out the door, tapping his foot and absolutely not saying a word. The big man finally yelled, "Would you cut that out!" to the white skinned invader. Who jumped back a foot or two and muttered, in a very poorly disguised gringo voice, "Donde esta el bano?"

The big man moaned, "Again. You've got to be kidding me? "

The white man shook his head, no. No he wasn't kidding. Why do you think he was tapping his foot?

So while the man with the Gringo accent went to the bathroom, the big man told the crowd, "I have an idea," laughing at his idea before he told the rest of them. "Why don't we...why don't we sign up this here Mayor for a game of Pelota . That's how the ancients used to settle their differences of opinion."

This idea scared the living shit out of the mayor, because he knew damn well Pelota was played to death, and he also knew damn well that it would be rigged so he would win. But before the mayor could fully react to that idea, the man with the strands of blond hair coming out of his mask, chirped in, "No, even better, we could sharpen his hands on Emiliano's stone, then troll for sharks."

The "Dad" got a cackle out of that idea, but added, "In case the sharks don't want to eat him, we could just leave him on the Black Sands Beach for a night, or two. Maybe we should bury him, up to his head, and see what happens."

More laughter, and finally, holding back, but wanting to get in on the fun, the "kid" innocently added, "Why don't we put him in one of those old fashioned...oh, what do you call them. The things where in the old days all you could see were his head and his hands. We could hold him hostage like that until we knew for sure that the Black Sands Resort can't be built. We could…"

But his Dad jumped in, "Great idea son. We'll hold him hostage. That's a great idea." Then turning to the rest of them, "I knew this kid had it in him. What do you think, guys. Let's hold on to this Pargo (he jabbed the machete into the bottom part of the Mayor's nose, accidentally letting out just a fine drop of blood) son-of-a-bitch until we know for sure the beach will be protected."

"That could be a long time?!" stammered the mayor, trying not to move his face, lest he cut more of the tip of his nose.

The "Dad" brought the machete down from the Mayor's face and pulled him up from the chair. The two other masked men went out front, checking to see if the coast was clear, while the "kid", now standing a little straighter, asked, "What are we gonna DO with him?"

"Well. I guess we can keep him at City Hall. That's where he belongs." And with that, the "Dad" pulled the Mayor towards the door.

Lola, not one to take sides when a machete was involved, calmly said, "Don't hurt him" then turned to her kids, and with a knowing eye said, "Hijos."

But they scampered out of the doorway and, as Adelante was gently ushered out the door, all Lola could think of was that she hadn't had time to disinfect his ear with a squirt of lime. And then, sadly, she thought, it might not really matter.

Not more than five minutes after they left, Martin, who had been in the bathroom all this time, came out and desperately searched the room. Everyone was gone. Lola had chased her kids out back. The other masked men had left with the mayor, towards city hall. And Martin, wondering how in the hell he had gotten into this situation in the first place, took off his mask and looked into the mirror and actually smiled at the crazed-eyed man that stared back at him.

What had he gotten himself into this time? How had he gotten into this mess? What fun!

Chapter 23

They were half way to City Hall, on foot, when they realized their other masked man, Martin, wasn't with them.

"Where in the hell is he?" Stan asked.

"Shit," moaned Gorde, "that Gringo is a pile of trouble."

"I didn't see him."

"Me either!"

"I think he's still in the bathroom," laughed Stan's son Rico, happy that there was somebody else to laugh at beside himself.

"Maybe he fell in love with himself and was having such a good time he forgot all about us," Craig howled, letting out a long hoot.

Everybody else cackled away, except for the Mayor, whom at this very moment had his head completely covered with one of the black masks, with the face side turned around so he couldn't see a thing.

They were coming up the hill, almost to Stan's place, and as they traveled, they were picking up a trail of onlookers: "Quien es?" "Who is it?" "What's going on?" everyone asked.

When the word got out that it was the mayor and that they were taking him to city hall under house arrest. Esmeralda had a long history of house arrests. It meant they weren't going to kill him right away. But it didn't especially mean he was completely off the hook. Over the years, some people had survived house arrest, and a few others, well, hadn't.

The whole town poured from their hammocks and, those who were working, from their jobs.

Nancy took one look out her window and shook her head. She noticed her husband at the head of the parade, limping along, but, she had to admit, not limping as much as usual. He must be having the time of his life, she thought, laughing to herself. And…Rico. Oh boy, she thought, Rico, a chip off his father's machete.

She was afraid, however, that if she didn't jump in and assert herself, her fear of another "Taxi Slaughter" type nightmare just might come true. So she waited until they passed by, assured that no harm was being done to the mayor and went directly over to speak with Adelante's wife Gloria.

When she got to Adelante's mansion she had a hard time getting in. And pacing out front, she cussed under her breath, "My husband is probably killing your husband, while your servants check to see if it's okay for them to let me in."

But the minute Gloria was told it was Nancy Lovejoy, she was out to the gate and apologizing for the inconvenience. She also knew that something must be up. Nancy, in fact anybody, for that matter, just didn't drop by for a chat.

"I think they were heading to city hall," Nancy assured Gloria.

"He wasn't hurt was he?"

"No. The whole town knows about it. He's under house arrest," Nancy reassured her.

And Gloria visibly relaxed, took a deep breath and then said, "Oh, I guess I should bring some food, que no. He might get a bit hungry and they're not going to let him out today, are they?"

"Probably not," Nancy answered matter of factly.

When the two women arrived, Adelante was in his office, with Stan, Craig, Rico and Gorde still wearing their masks. Nancy and Gloria entered, with Nancy pointing to the masks, "Aren't those things a little hot boys?"

Nobody wanted to answer, but the mayor did, saying, "Yes. Can you get me out of this thing?"

Nancy turned to her husband, her son, Gorde and Craig and shrugged her shoulders, as if to say, why not? Who's fooling anybody here anyway? But the guys didn't want to take off their masks, although they let the mayor take off his.

"Here's the deal," Stan said, no longer disguising his voice. "All we want is total assurance that the Black Sand Beach deal is dead, the turtles will not be bothered and that Nando will get to live out his life in peace. That's all we want. You've had a good run in this town. I know we've not seen eye to eye on a lot of things. But this one, this one is a biggie my friend, in case you hadn't noticed, and the people want some real assurances. And it can't be your normal hot air crap. We want it from the Feds too. And until we get it, you're going to have to live here, under house arrest."

When the mayor heard the words, the people, he knew he was in deep shit. When he heard the Feds he felt suddenly weak. He peeked outside and saw over one hundred men milling around, casually holding onto their machetes. Each machete, even the old ones, had a bright, shiny new edge on it, courtesy of Emiliano Vargas. They were outside of their sheathes, which wasn't the normal way they were carried around town, and that could mean only one thing—they meant business.

Stan, proud that he had stated their case so clearly, rested his case. All the other masked men nodded their heads in agreement. With that, Stan, seeing that Gloria had brought some food, added, "Let's let him have some time to think about it…with his wife," and Stan along with his wife and his masked gang of banditos, slowly walked out of the mayors office.

When they got outside, Nancy was about to reprimand them for creating a dangerous situation in the town when they all took off their masks and started giggling like a bunch of teenagers on laughing gas.

"Did you see his face when I put that machete up to his hooked little beak?" Stan gasped out between breaths. "My god that thing is sharp. I think I nicked him accidentally."

They were all doubled over in laughter, Gorde wheezing a little, Craig's face turning red, Stan walking without a limp for the first time in sixty years.

"No, no. What I liked best was when Rico said, "Dad, We can't do THAT!" chuckled Gorde.

Rico blushed, hugged his father and said, "Sorry Pop. I wasn't thinking."

"It's okay son. You were great!"

Craig Galetas looked around, smiled and said, "Where do you think our friend Martin is, huh?"

This started another round of laughter and Nancy, seeing that the guys really weren't in a dangerous mood at all, softly questioned, "What the hell happened, anyway?"

Chapter 24

In the days after Adelante's house arrest the Tranquilleno household had quickly turned into Esmeralda's unofficial war room. And a now sober Gorde, who much to the amazement of even himself, had not taken a single drink since hearing the rumor that the mainland was going to invade Esmeralda and physically take over the island.

Gorde now plotted with his compadres on how to thwart the invasion. He sat on his back patio with Craig Galetas and his monkey Mickey, Stan and Nancy Lovejoy, Stan's son Rico (who was getting more and more involved in the action since his masked bandito stint). Gorde's mom Magda was there too, mostly because she was so concerned about her son's non-drinking problem. She had even stopped pelting passersby. Henry Ortiz was present, as well as Paulo Gabernetti, Vicente Hernandez (they each brought about a dozen of their drivers). Antonio Vargas, who thankfully hadn't brought his Dad, and Martin Slate, who walked in sporting a goatee, which caused quite a ruckus.

"You're looking like Van Gough, or is that Van Dyke," hollered Stan.

"No, I think he looks like that Tennis player dude," Rico barked. "Agassi."

"I like it," exclaimed Gorde's wife Vicki as she served up glasses of sangrita, tequila and limes.

"I think it makes you look more mature."

"Ya, like the Professor needs to look mature," Craig chirped in.

They'd been calling Martin the professor since they found out about his patents and inventions. Paulo and Vicente agreed that they liked the goat. Antonio, Henry, Nancy and Magda were neutral. Whatever the case, Martin, with his new goat and tanned skin cut quite a dashing figure for an ex-engineer from Portland, Oregon.

When the chatter settled down, Gorde took the floor: "Okay, okay. Let's talk through what our options are. If we can take a strong stand maybe we can discourage them. And besides, I don't think any of us can just lay down while the mainlanders come and invade our island, que no."

"I second the motion," Stan hollered from the back.

"Do you have any ideas?" Gorde questioned.

But Stan started talking to Craig and Magda about a new kind of ice cream he was trying to develop. So Gorde turned to the crowd, hoping someone would come up with an idea.

"Maybe we could blockade the harbor," Vicki volunteered. "I bet they'll try to land in the harbor. It's the safest route." Vicki turned to Antonio Vargas, who was thinking, scratching his head. He looked up and mumbled, "How?"

For a good minute nobody spoke, then Magda, the queen of torture, piped in, "paper mache?"

"Oh mama, what are you thinking," Gorde laughed. "What are we gonna do with Paper Mache."

"Why not," she protested, "we make paper mache bombs, paint them with a waterproof cover. What will they know?!"

"Humm."

"Good idea."

"It'll scare the hell out of them!"

Then Rico jumped in with, "I could rig a few to go off. You know, using my M-80's and a fuse, so they'd think they were real."

The crowd was starting to wake up a bit with this idea.

"Okay," Gorde agreed, "Let's start making as many as we can. Maybe we can get the word out to Hermana."

Antonio Vargas volunteered, "We can varnish them at my place. We have the space and the varnish."

"Okay. Mom, Antonio, Rico. Go, get as many of them as you can in the harbor. Vamanos! We only have two days."

And off they ran, well, Magda walked her usual crawl, slow motion walk, but Antonio went home to set up the production area and Rico started off to Hermana for help.

"Any other ideas?" Gorde asked.

"I sent out a press-release over the Internet telling the whole world about the U.S./Mexico invasion plan. That should embarrass them into submission," Martin joked.

Gorde looked up at Martin. He wasn't sure what the Internet was, and said, "Great."

He looked up at Stan and Craig in the far corner, gabbing away, and Gorde, a little pissed they weren't taking the meeting too seriously, yelled out, "Hey Stan. Craig. What's going on? This is serious stuff. Wake up!"

Both Craig and Stan simultaneously said, "Fuck you."

Then Craig stood up, "I have an idea. If we use this fake bomb thing, maybe we could also do a few for me, to carry in the flyin' machine. We could fill them with cocos or something. Let me tell you, if that ever hit anyone, they'd be offed."

Gorde turned and looked up to the sky, "Ijole. Guys. This is serious stuff. We can't joke around. Do you understand?"

"Who's joking," Craig protested, "I'm as serious as the honey is strong."

The Stan stood up. "He'd be a great diversion. What harm could it do?"

"You two are serious?!"

They nodded, Stan and Craig both sporting silly grins, yet determined to convince everyone their idea could work.

"Okay. If you think it will help," Gorde conceded.

Paulo and Vicente now stood up, cleared their throats in unison, then Paulo began; "We have men. These good men," he pointed to all the drivers, some of them pretty tough looking, especially Paulo's drivers, and others, mostly Vicente's men, family men.

Vicente continued, "Do with them what you will. We all know, over the years, that our drivers have proven to know how to use the sharp side of a machete."

This got the crowd laughing and throwing out lines like, "Ya, maybe we can slaughter a few mainlanders this time, rather than our own."

"Maybe if they try and take our taxi territories we'll win."

"Put them in a few of Reliable's cars and they won't be invading Esmeralda for generations, cause they'll never arrive."

"What are you saying?" a Reliable driver countered.

"I'm saying your cars stink. And you stink," yelled back the Central Taxi driver who had made the initial comment.

And before they knew it, voices were raising. Machete blades could be seen flashing in the sunlight. Gorde, who was now realizing that he had lost the crowd, and probably, he thought, lost the war before they even got a chance to fight the damn thing, reached back behind his counter, found his gun and shot it three times in the air.

All was silent.

"You burros! If we fight each other, we'll surely lose the island," Gorde pleaded.

"He's right," Stan said, "Vicente, Paulo. You two either have to work together on this, or, if that doesn't work, just stay in your own areas and do what you can do."

"We'll work it out. But what are we gonna do?" Vicente pleaded. "What is our plan?"

After a good five minutes of mumbling but no solid answers, Vicki again came forward and said, "Let's just take care of them. Why fight them. Why don't we feed them tamales, plantains, honey. That should calm them down. Why fight them?"

Everyone turned to each other. What kind of war would that be. Greeting the enemy with food and entertaining them.

"And, of course," she said with a broad wink of an eye, "once they drink the water, they will never be the same."

"I'll second THAT motion," Martin yelled, rubbing his new goatee.

Again the crowd laughed, because, it was true. It took a good year before a mainlander could get used to the organisms in the water. Just like Martin, anyone who stayed on the island, drank the water and ate the food, was bound to get a strong case of turistas—fever, weak, diarrhea. Usually, at first, it was so strong they'd think they were dying. Then, as the weeks and months passed by, it was just flu-like symptoms, and after a half a year, it was mild, slowly going away.

So, maybe Vicki had something. They could greet the invaders with food and water and let nature take its course. Many other ideas were discussed and the islanders, not ones to worry about time, forgot that the invasion was in only two days. So, while a large part of the power brokers of Esmeralda sat in a meeting, drinking and laughing and plotting, the press, having recently been alerted to "the invasion" rumor through Martin's e-mail, were on internet time and made plans for their own invasion of sorts.

Chapter 25

Maria Valasquez Romero Vargas ran a small, four-hammock, three-table palapa restaurant on the fisherman's beach. She had been tromping around the fishermen's beach since the day she was born, some fifty-seven odd years ago, and she knew her fish. Every morning her fisherman husband Antonio Vargas (the village's one and only expert fisherman/triathlete/cock fighter) would pull in his well-worn, eighteen-foot skiff overflowing with shrimp, lobster, octopus, tuna, and the assorted pargo, shark, sometimes even pez bella or marlin.

It was a ritual both knew well. Antonio would run his engine hard directly toward the sandy shore. Then at the very last second tuck his outboard and literally fly up the sand bluff, as fast as he could, until the boat came crashing to a squirrelly stop, kind of like birds that don't know how to land on terra firma. Maria would calmly walk out of the palapa, inspecting each and every fish like a world-class diamond buyer, tossing a few of the choicest into her basket. The rest went to the market, or the hotel, or to Hermana. Then she would start her long and ritualistic preparation of her famous fish dishes.

On this particular morning, the morning after Martin had sent his E-mail to the press warning against a possible invasion of the island, Maria sat in her palapa kitchen, chopping onions, listening to the melody of the beautiful blackbirds called Sanate.

Tall, slender, fork-tailed, and completely black, their song chirped of tropical paradise, a relaxed, high-pitched serenade Maria absolutely adored. The mist off the ocean softly blew on-shore, creating a fine, subtle rainbow-like effect to the left of her, hovering in the air between the water and her palapa.

Maria's palapa sported a rather interesting collection of shoes. The whole roof was piled with sandals and shoes in various states of deterioration. It was a well-known tradition at this Ellis Island Gateway of Esmeralda, to take off a person's shoes, much like the Japanese do upon entering their home. But on the island of Esmeralda, they threw their shoes on top of Maria's palapa. For many it signified freedom from the rigors of mainland life. For Maria, it meant her packed dirt floors would remain unmarred by the rough-bottomed shoes of the modern world.

"A pair of those hard shoes on my floor, can completely ruin years of watering and packing," Maria normally told her customers who forgot to take off their shoes.

Maria chopped in silence as the sun came over the cliff side. The beach was completely quiet, not another soul for miles…and then, breaking the silence from far off in the distance was a small flotilla of boats, lined up about fifty yards apart entered the harbor. First a twenty foot boat, then a couple of twenty-five footers right behind them, and finally, another twenty footer. Five in all, each carrying a two-person camera crew from a different mainland TV station. Antonio came right in behind them with a stern look on his face.

The Journalists had all come in private boats, so they left their gear on the boats and came up toward Maria's palapa. There was a crew from Los Angeles, one from New York, one from Washington, and two from Mexico City.

Antonio had been intercepting them, telling them they could only come in with his guidance. And now, since five was all they thought would be coming, they were allowed to land. Antonio instructed them to take off their shoes and the journalists happily complied.

"I have never, ever heard of this," exclaimed Stephanie Chung, the reporter from Los Angeles. "It reminds me of a country version of Japan. Cool."

Stephanie's cameraman, Roger Wistrand, who was particularly well-traveled nodded his head in agreement, "Me neither."

Within a few minutes they were all situated comfortably under Maria's palapa waiting for the press briefing that had been promised in the E-mail. Maria had been instructed by Martin to carefully prepare all meals for the journalists, taking extra care to soak the vegetables in Microdyn (a solution that killed all the micro-organisms that tended to wreak havoc on one's intestines).

"They are our allies," Martin had told her and Antonio. "They will accomplish more than all our other schemes of flying contraptions, fake bombs and what-not. They just might be what Nando's vision was about, when he saw us winning the battle by exposing our battle to the universe."

So now, Maria, flashed her big gold-toothed smile, thanked the journalists for taking off their shoes and prepared a hearty meal. Meanwhile, Martin prepared something else for the journalists, a speech, one that he hoped would get the whole world on the island's side.

Still in his room, Martin struggled with his words, hoping he had covered all he had wished to say. By one o'clock he had arrived at the palapa, carrying his hand-written speech, with his face covered with the black mask (the very same one he used during the Adelante escapade). After introducing himself to the crew as the spokesperson of the people of Esmeralda, he moved to a table at the far end of Maria's palapa and when all the cameras and microphones were ready he began.

"We the people of Esmeralda request that the governments of Mexico and the United States respect our sovereign shores. We have been alerted to the possibility of an invasion, in which an innocent culture could be destroyed; a culture that has survived from the days of the Zapotecs. A culture that has many important advances we could learn from, including, an ancient man who has lived for over one hundred and thirty years, who is a living museum of knowledge that should be preserved. His customs and traditions hold the key to longevity. He is one hundred and thirty-one years old, with a body and a mind as fit as most sixty-year-olds on the mainland. And he is the protector of a rare leatherback turtle, which, if these governments have their way, will become extinct. All we ask is that the world community take a good look at this man, at this beach and the turtles, before they are destroyed. Thank you."

Martin sat down and the hands went up, and the questions came fast and furious.

"Where is this man?

"How do we know he is 131 years old?"

"What kind of turtles?"

"Can we get an interview with the Zapotec?"

Martin raised his hands to calm them down and said, "He lives nearby and when the time is right you will be allowed to see him. Right now, we're extremely concerned for his safety. We know he is over one hundred because he knows many, many things about the ancient cultures. He remembers the Mexican Revolution like it was yesterday, even though he has never read a book, never seen a TV or never listened to a radio."

"How did the island find out about the planned invasion?"

"I can't answer that," Martin mumbled, suddenly feeling self conscious, suddenly seeing the cameras and the lights and imagining what he would look like on TV with a black mask covering His face.

"That's all for now," Martin said while he got up and headed out the side door.

The reporters started to give chase, but Martin turned around, stared them down and without a word, they got the message.

Meanwhile, the islanders prepped for war. Back at Craig Galetas's place, Craig and Mickey were practicing with the flying machine.

Craig was trying to train Mickey to drop coconuts on demand. While still on the ground, he handed Mickey a bag with four coconuts, and pretended like he was flying the machine. Then he turned to Mickey and yelled, "Now."

Mickey just looked at Craig, wondering what the hell he wanted. Frustrated, Craig went over to where Mickey was, took the bag and the coconuts, sat Mickey in the pilot's seat and returned to where he had positioned Mickey. Again, Craig yelled "Now". This time, he threw the coconut out over the side. He yelled "now" again and threw another coconut.

It took Craig nearly three hours to get Mickey to comply and then, finally, something clicked in the little monkey's brain and he had it down pat. Craig yelled "now", Mickey threw the coconut. Perfect. He was ready for a test run.

He started up his flying machine, a combination of a fan, a sail and a reworked shopping cart. He stacked 4 coconuts in the basket, tied Mickey in, making sure that if Mickey did get a little nuts, at least he wouldn't fall into the ocean, and, off they flew. Using the cliffs right out front of Craig's, along with the incoming breeze, they lifted off into the clear blue skies of Esmeralda.

Within a minute Craig was out over the fishing harbor. He could see the beautiful crescent shaped bay that had protected Esmeralda from storms for generations, he could even make out Maria's little palapa. It was time to see if Mickey had the right stuff. It was time to see if they could hit a moving target. But what? They didn't want to hurt any of their friends, and a coconut, dropped from a few thousand feet up, could be a lethal weapon. So, they decided to drop them in the oyster floats, which were inflated tires that floated near the north side of the bay where the oystermen dove for the hard-shelled delicacies.

Craig circled the three inflated inner tubes three times to make sure nobody was underneath, then, on the fourth pass, signaled to Mickey to let her go with a, "Now". Mickey, who had done an admiral job on land, couldn't quite hear Craig over the engine. Again, he yelled, "Now" this time pointing to the target. Nothing.

Oh man, thought Craig, I'm up here with the world's stupidest monkey. Maybe I should let him drive, that way, I could drop the bombs. Then he stopped, thought again about what he had just thought about, and surmised that he must be the world's stupidest person, to even think about letting a monkey drive his flying machine.

But, two hours later, with a change of command, it seemed to work. Mickey flew in a circle, Craig dropped coconuts. They hit three out of three in the inner tubes. The only problem was, to land, Craig had to get back into the controls. This was quit a feat. The flyin' machine was essentially designed for one person, not one person and a crazy monkey that took poor directions.

On their way home, after their second run, Craig found out how hard it was to change back. He tried to get Mickey to come to the left side of the cage, with the idea that he could simultaneously jump to the right side. But when he gave the signal to jump and yelled "now" Mickey just looked at him and dropped a coconut. Craig jumped to the right, threw the flyin' machine off balance, and they started to lose altitude— something that you just did not want to do when you're using a small fan, a parachute and luck to stay up in the air.

Finally, with Mickey protesting every second of the way, Craig just grabbed the monkey, threw him back into the basket and took control of the steadily falling aircraft, probably just in time to avert a disastrous brush with the Pacific, and maybe, death. Craig turned the fan to full power, tweaked the controls to give him some lift and within a minute or two they were high in the air, on their way home. I guess it'll do in wartime, thought Craig, but I'm definitely not going to make a habit of letting Mickey on the controls.

Meanwhile, back at Gorde Tranquellino's place, Magda and over thirty women from Esmeralda and Hermana were furiously finishing up their paper mache bombs. They were about the size of a basketball, with about a dozen little pointy ends that simulated a bomb that Stan had drawn for them.

Gorde was amazed at how real the gray bombs looked, "They're going to scare them right out of their boats!"

"Wait till we set them off," Stan's son Rico bragged, "We're putting puca shells inside so it looks like shrapnel."

The next day, after Martin's speech ran on the five TV stations, and as the story broke, many other stations purchased the footage and most of the world heard the news. Soon, the island was inundated with over thirty camera crews.

At first, Antonio and all his fishermen friends kept the herds under control, bringing them in, asking them to check in with Maria, take off their shoes, talk to Martin. But then, as more and more boats arrived, they had a hard time keeping the boats under control, and finally, it was a free-for-all. The boaters lost their patience and started blasting by Antonio's barricade.

The villagers, seeing that Antonio was being overrun, mistakenly thought the real invasion had begun and pulled out their bag of tricks. All the fake bombs were put into place. As the boats blasted past Antonio and the other fishermen, the floating bombs looked real and they realized that, yes, they were in a war zone.

And when Rico started to set them off, well, there was some pretty interesting footage being shot. Steel gray bombs, in little Esmeralda harbor, exploding and blowing shrapnel all over the place. In the midst of all this, someone tried to land a plane on the highway out by Craig Galetas' place. And that's when Craig and his co-pilot, bombardier Mickey, swung into action.

Their test run had gone okay, but this was the real thing. And Mickey, Craig soon found, had learned from watching Craig on the test run and had a real knack for dropping the coconut filled bombs right into boats.

Martin looked out and saw the bombs go off, saw Mickey high overhead plopping coconut-filled bombs on innocent journalists, and realized that if they weren't careful, they might just lose this war, before it even started.

"We need to do something about this before it gets completely out of hand," Martin moaned to his new ally Stan. "Why don't we just feed them, water them down and let nature take its course."

"They're not respecting our privacy," Stan countered. "They've been just blasting past Antonio with rude gestures. Look, some of them are not taking off their shoes when Maria asks them to."

"You're right," Martin agreed, and he turned to Maria and said, "just the ones in their barefeet, the rest, feed them your normal fare."

Within twenty-four hours, there were a lot of journalist walking around Esmeralda with modern shoes and an old fashioned case of the turistas. Soon, their ranks thinned considerably, with many returning to the mainland to visit hospitals to straighten out their twisted and painful intestinal tracts.

Still, the news was out. All around the globe footage was being broadcast of Esmeralda and their plight. People in Kansas saw the bombs going off, the shrapnel flying through the air. One station actually showed a shot of Craig and his flying machine, saying it was this lone eccentric man with his monkey, against the United States and Mexico. And the flying machine had won!

Soon the name of Esmeralda was on the lips of anyone that watched TV or read a newspaper. The presidents of the United States of America and the United States of Mexico made urgent phone calls back and forth, just to make sure neither one of them had actually attacked this out of the way island.

Not more than five minutes after the conversation a terse statement from their spokespeople announced there had never been an invasion. Both announced they would further study the ancient man and the turtle issue and there would be no invasion, period.

And that was it! Finito.

Alfredo Lopez Ramos, the real estate investor who had been sure he was going to successfully push this project through, was sitting in his home in Mexico city when he saw the news. He nearly blew a blood vessel.

"What has come of this world, when a little piss ant island is telling the U.S. and Mexico what to do. I…I can't take this. They should go in there and blow those mothers right off our beach."

He stomped around, his neck getting red, his gold chains chattering away, and finally, he just went off, "I'll do it myself. I'll do it myself."

And with that, he packed up his gun, gassed up his Cadillac and left toward Esmeralda, ready for war.

Chapter 26

Again, it seemed the village of Esmeralda had beat the odds. Again, they had somehow stumbled out of a tough situation against the mainland, intact. When word quickly spread of their victory over the mainland, Stan Lovejoy, with a little wry smile, declared the following three days, January thirteen, fourteen and fifteen a "National Holiday".

"Why not," Stan laughed, "If Nando can dance everyday of his life, and I must say, he's had a long one, why not have a three day celebration? We deserve it!"

"We should give our holiday a name," Nancy suggested, "how about Esmeralda Days." Stan loved it. From that moment on, January thirteen, fourteen and fifteen were a national holiday on the tiny island of Esmeralda. An island which was now on the map but still not a nation.

The men congregated at Gorde's place, after two long days of staying dry, he picked up a jug of tequila that must of been a full liter and tipped it to his friends, "Viva La Esmeralda."

Once the news of the bi-country announcement had sunk in and most of the reporters had fled the island, things began to get back to normal. Day one of "Esmeralda Days" ended with a beautiful sunset and lots of clouds to watch.

Even Henry Ortiz, who had worked himself out of a job, but into the good graces of the village, saw images in the clouds. For Henry, who had been worrying lately how he was actually going to feed his family when his meager savings ran out, saw huge mangoes and pineapple. When his wife Melda saw them too, and then his kids, jumping up and down, laughing, said they saw them too, Henry knew that he was going to be a mango/pineapple farmer.

It was a night to remember for many people. Most couldn't recall when they'd had a better sunset. Antonio Vargas and his whole family had spotted a marlin in the clouds. A good omen. Nearly every time they had seen a fish like that in the clouds, the very next day, they had caught one. So now, pointing to the sky, jumping up and down, hootin' and hollerin', the Vargas clan was not only celebrating Esmeralda Days, but their coming good fortune.

Of course, Paulo, Vicente and Stan, hanging together, taking a sip of Tequila and Sangrita, looked up at all the pretty colors and saw just that, a bunch of pretty colors. For the life of them, they couldn't find a bee for a barn.

"Look Dad," Vicente's youngest said, pointing to the sky, "It's a star…or, a well, a badge or something. Do you see it. Do you?"

He didn't see it but he did see that the village was back to normal. Over on the sea wall, most of the Jefe rats had returned to their sunset sentry. Some said even the Jefes played Cloud Games, and Vicente, staring over there at this minute, might be inclined to agree. The rats were looking up at the clouds, squeaking and acting, well, just about the same as the rest of the islanders.

After the sunset was gone, and all the colors had drained from the sky, the whole crowd turned to listen to the squeaking, squashing, huffing and puffing sound of two U.S. Navy frogmen as they clamored up the sand, apparently on special assignment to help with the "invasion" of Esmeralda.

Gorde stood over them in a friendly yet still fairly menacing posture. "Would you two like to join us for dinner?"

They stayed, for a full hour, sitting between Gorde and Stan, both backed up by half a dozen smiling, happy-go-lucky islanders who had their machetes still in their holders. And the two men, after eating through weak smiles (like they'd sat on a tack or had a corncob up their back) asked if they could be excused like four-year-olds at Christmas Dinner.

When Stan said, "Sure, looks like a good night for a swim," they walked back out, escorted by a dozen or so men, and, swam back out to God knows where, to do God knows what.

Chapter 27

Nando had gone up to the temples to thank the turtle Gods for their guidance, for their vision, for their continued support. And now, back in his cave, he painted his body with red, blue, orange, purple and yellow pigments, dabbing little dots all over his body so he looked like a spotted leopard.

Below day two of Esmeralda Days was about to begin. Since it was being held on Nando's beach and some people couldn't make the long walk across the island, the crowd was a little smaller. Some people, like Stan, made it, even though they probably shouldn't have even tried.

The idea had been to walk the paths, singing the songs of both villages. Most everyone who walked knew the songs, even Stan. But Stan spent most of his time cussing at his bad leg, cause the pain had returned with a vengeance. Nancy spent most of her time trying to shut up her husband, or at least get him to clean up his language. Stan was still cussing, yelling and wondering why he didn't just take a boat, when they arrived at Nando's bay.

Nando agreed to be a part of the celebrations by dancing a few of the older traditional dances that most people who were now on the beach had forgotten.

"After all," Stan had said to Nando, "we wouldn't be an island without the guidance of the turtles. And it goes without saying that without you, we would no longer have a connection to their wisdom. You and your beach would be a wonderful addition to our ceremony. As you know, these last couple of days will probably become a part of our tradition, like the three turtles."

What could Nando say? Si. Of course! Nando liked the idea of teaching some of the younger people his dances. He figured that way, when it was time for him to go into the mountains, the traditions would live on.

"Why not teach the whole village," Martin had added. "That way, we're assured that someone will take up the dances with a daily passion."

So now a whole crowd of villagers, from both sides of the island, waited in anticipation. They sat in a semi-circle at the base of Nando's soft sand trail. The very same one he had used for decades to roll down to the beach.

High above, Nando waited for his body paint to dry. He wasn't really sure if he was ready. There were a lot of people down there. More people than he had ever seen in one place, at one time. But he looked down, saw the children and wanted above all, to find one person out of the crowd that would take over his turtle sentry when it was time for him to go up the hill.

He tucked and rolled. Nando could hear the crowd begin to roar. And when he landed, the village was on its feet, applauding and cheering. Nando, using all his years of experience to dance the ancient story of the turtles, was accompanied by Martin whom played the drums as best he could. After the first dance was complete, Martin made a little speech, telling the crowd that Nando and he had put together a special new dance, one that would commemorate the victory over the mainland.

As the crowd watched in awe, Martin and Nando danced the story of the prior week. They showed Martin coming to the Black Sand Beach, danced the burning of Stan's hut (complete with fire sound effects), told of flying machines and dropping coconuts, bombs in the water, even E-mail with a laptop. When they were done, after the crowd stopped cheering, Nando asked if anyone wanted to learn a dance. He would be teaching a simple dance that could be learned, the Spring Dance.

For a long moment nobody responded and Nando, thinking that he probably would be the last of his dying breed, let his head drop. He stared at the sand. But Martin nudged him to look up and when he did lines were forming right in front of him. These lines were almost as long as the tequila lines at the annual Tequila and CockFights. And Nando, hoping to find a successor, smiled at the long line and thanked the Turtle Gods for their continued support.

In the afternoon, Martin and a few other people waited around while Nando swam out and found an adult turtle. Nando guided him back to shore and anyone who wanted to could come up and take a closer look at the animal. When Nando rolled the turtle over, Martin questioned him about the small emerald-blue dot in the middle of the turtle's underside.

"Oh, they've always had that," Nando assured Martin. "Nothing new."

Martin had never seen anything in the books about the blue spot and in the last couple of weeks, he'd done extensive research on the turtles. It was his way of going to war. And this little blue dot, he thought, just might be the kind of information he needed to save these turtles. He would have to check that out.

And then there was Alfredo Lopez Ramos, who had come to the Island ready for war, and had arrived on the wrong side of the island, at the wrong time of day. He had entered a ghost town of a village, wondering if indeed the island had been taken over, and all the people had left, and the world just hadn't been told.

"Where is everybody?" he asked to the people who hadn't gone to the celebration.

"I don't know. No se" was all he heard, over and over and over, until finally, so frustrated that he knew they were lying to him, he left the island, hoping to come up with a plan to take some kind of action into his own hands.

Chapter 28

Day three of "Esmeralda Days" began with a beautiful sunrise. Everyone on the island was celebrating by showing off his or her "armed forces" in the tradition of the now defunct Russian Empire. Craig Galetas was giving rides in his flyin' machine.

"Come on Hijo," Gorde begged, "I won't even bring any coconuts."

"I don't know Gorde. It might not make it," Craig replied.

"Owwww come on. What's the worst that can happen?"

So off they went, over the beautiful calm, early morning waters of the Pacific. Sputtering away with Craig at the controls pushing for all the lift he could muster, with his fan at full throttle, searching for a trace of on-shore breeze to give them enough lift to get Gorde off the ground. Up they sputtered, barely above the water, when from around the far end of the point came a helicopter. Craig barely had time to adjust his lift when the copter was on him, and desperate to get away from the spinning blades, he turned off his fan and let go of his controls, which dropped him down just enough to clear the renegade copter.

Problem was, once the helicopter had passed, Craig, with all his might, couldn't get control of his flyin' machine and Craig, his fan, his parachute and, of course, all two hundred and fifty-eight pounds of Gorde, headed for the blue Pacific. The parachute slowed them down just enough to have time to abandon ship.

"Jump Gorde, jump."

"What are you crazy? Fly this thing."

"We're not gonna make it. Jump so you'll be clear of the chute and the engine."

Gorde, holding on for dear life, just couldn't let go of the security of the flyin' machine. Craig realized this and figuring things would probably be a lot better off without both of them pushing the machine into the water, prepared to jump.

"Gorde. I'm telling you. You gotta jump."

The big man just shook his head. They were just seconds from the water now. He wasn't going to let go.

"Okay. I'm jumping," Craig yelled. "Good luck. At impact you're going to get a little banged up with the cage."

And just as Craig jumped away from the flyin' machine, Gorde realized he didn't want to be alone in the cage when they hit. So he reached out, grabbed Craig's leg and held on for dear life.

"Gorde. Gorde. Let go. What the fuck!"

Gorde pulling on Craig's leg had completely changed the direction of their descent. Suddenly, they had lift, suddenly, they were hovering over the water, not falling like a dead weight. Their rate of descent was slowed down so much they actually had time to jump away from the cage, just before impact.

"Ijole," Gorde yelled as he hit the water, "I haven't had this much fun since Bromista was lost in the canyon."

"Did you see who it was?" Craig shouted, "they could have gotten us killed."

"No. Is your machine gonna be okay?"

"I don't know. I think so."

And the boats were there before Gorde's hair got wet. Antonio Vargas was the first. He had been tracking them before they even hit water.

"It wasn't the air force," Antonio shouted as he pulled them in. "It looked like a private copter."

"Then who the hell was that?" asked Craig.

For his part, Alfredo Lopez Ramos, who hadn't flown this type of helicopter before, was struggling to get used to the new type of controls. He'd headed back to the mainland and come up with a plan to come back with the copter, swing down the coast to the black sand beach and take care of business himself. The problem was, he was having a hard time with this modern copter. He hadn't flown in fifteen years.

Now, rounding the bend close to the Black Sands Beach, he was struggling with landing. He was glad there wasn't a wind, because he knew from his years of flying experience that with a wind, and his lack of command on the controls, that he'd never be able to make it.

He set her down on the north side of the beach. Coming out of the helicopter with his gun drawn, Alfredo immediately saw him. He stood above the beach near a cave. Painted from head to toe in bright reds and blues with a few dashes of yellow, the man was little. What's the big deal? thought Alfredo. This guy can't be more than five feet tall.

Nando didn't move. Alfredo wasn't sure if he just didn't see him, or if it was a trick, so he kept his gun pointed directly at him as he moved in for a closer look. Alfredo soon realized the Indian's eyes were half shut and now, as he got even closer, he could hear the chanting. A soft, low chanting.

"Hum. Bow. Ahhh. Ya. Hum Bow. Ahh. Yo."

Alfredo walked right up the steep, soft-sand path, keeping his eyes glued to the Indian's face. Nothing. A sitting duck, thought Alfredo. So he moved even closer, raised his gun, pointing it at the Indian's right leg and fired.

What happened next surprised the desperate and angry gun toting realtor more than anything he had ever seen in his life—and Alfredo had seen, and he had done, an awful lot. What happened next, Alfredo had later told his friends back home, was impossible.

Alfredo saw the bullet go right into the Indian's right leg above the kneecap. He saw the skin part, the blood splatter. The Indian didn't even flinch. Not one bit of reaction. Not even an eye flutter. It was if he were in another world.

Alfredo stood there, in shock, for a long, long moment. And then, slowly, Nando opened his eyes, smiled at Alfredo, kept on chanting, took a small jar of honey-like substance out, rubbed a little on his wound and slowly closed his eyes again.

And that's when Alfredo noticed it. He looked down at the Indian's right leg and saw that the wound had stopped bleeding. Then, before his very eyes, he saw it begin to heal.

This is like a time-lapse photography trick, thought Alfredo. This can't be happening. He stared as the wound closed and after what seemed like a minute or two, he couldn't be sure because he was in a state of shock, the wound slowly turned into a scar. Nothing more remained. Alfredo thought of shooting the Indian again, but decided it might be safer to just grab him, get him in the helicopter and get the hell off the island. Alfredo came up behind him and picked the Indian up like he was a piece of furniture, tossed the stiff Indian over his shoulder and began to trudge down the soft sand trail. The Indian offered no resistance. He just smiled.

When they reached the copter Alfredo was amazed how light the man was and how easily he could be lifted into the passenger seat. Still he hadn't moved much and Alfredo wondered why. In the driver's side now, Alfredo saw the handcuffs he had brought along for good measure said, "Just in case you get an ideas," while he cuffed Nando's arms behind his back.

What a strange little man, thought Alfredo. Hasn't said a word. Painted with spots. How in the hell had that wound healed so fast? What was in the jar?

They flew for a good twenty minutes toward the mainland, when suddenly and without warning, the Indian jumped out of the helicopter, flying silently through the air, arms cuffed behind his back, to a certain death.

"Hey. Hey. What the...hell?" Alfredo, taken completely by surprise, turned his craft around and circled the water where the Indian should have landed. He couldn't see a thing. Maybe he just dropped straight to the bottom. He was cuffed, thought Alfredo. That solves one problem. Don't have to worry what to do with him. What a nut!

Martin knew that the helicopter that nearly clipped Craig and Gorde was bad news the minute he saw it and immediately got on the phone, searching to see who had rented copters this day and when he heard Alfredo's name he knew something big was up. He asked the owner to hold onto Alfredo if he arrived in the next couple of hours and asked Antonio to get him to the Black Sands Beach right away.

Of course, when Antonio heard why he urgently needed to get to the other side of the island, thirteen other men felt as if they had to go also, just as a matter of support. So, they all loaded up, quickly drove to Nando's beach and saw the blood drops on the sand near his cave.

Martin went into overdrive, giving everyone orders, telling two men to take the trail. Two more men were directed to check the temple, two more to take the main road and the rest of them were going to the helicopter rental office...on the double.

When Alfredo arrived at the airport, he was asked if he had any trouble with the helicopter. He told them no, although the technology was a little over his head, it worked fine. The owner asked him to wait around, saying the mechanic had noticed the blades were a bit bent. Alfredo thought nothing of it. In fact, the owner asked him if he wanted to have lunch brought in and Alfredo, thinking that it was a nice gesture, said sure.

So when Martin and eight machete-welding villagers arrived at the airport, the owner told them Alfredo was in the back office, having lunch. Martin went in first. Alfredo was in mid-bite and almost choked on his sandwich.

"Where is he?" Martin barked.

"Why the fuck are you here?" Alfredo said, stuttering on the F.

"Tell me where Nando is?" Martin managed to spit out through his ever-tightening jaws. "Now!"

"I can't help you pal. He's a nut. He jumped right out of my copter."

Martin squeezed the realtor's arm tightly, using his other hand to grab the thick gold chain around his neck, using it like a choke chain on a dog, and pulled him out toward the helicopter.

"Hey. I didn't push him. He jumped."

The gold chain broke from the pressure, spraying the tarmac with golden links. Alfredo wanted to pick them up but Martin held him firm and fighting the urge to kill this slime right now, said, "You gotta show me where."

Soon, they were up in the air, circling the area where Nando had jumped, Alfredo flying, Martin sitting next to Antonio who was holding a machete to the realtor's neck and commanding, "Are you sure? You're certain? This is it?"

"It's a big ocean. But this is the general area," Alfredo said, then, hoping this new piece of information wouldn't startle the big man holding the blade to his neck, he said, "He was cuffed."

"Handcuffed," Martin muttered.

"Yeah."

They flew for another five minutes and when Martin saw the boats had started to catch up with them, he looked Alfredo right in the eye and said, "Jump".

"Come again. What?"

"Jump, or he's gonna slit your throat right here," and Martin, realizing this man didn't believe him, nodded to Antonio, who pressed the blade to Alfredo's neck and drew blood.

This convinced Alfredo he meant business. Martin took the controls from Alfredo and gave him a shove.

Alfredo took the plunge, falling five, maybe six hundred feet and much to his surprise, when he landed, he only had a broken leg and a bad shoulder (at least that's what he thought they were). But he was lucky enough to have survived. What he didn't have was exceptional luck, because the first boat to pick him up was Antonio's, with his brother at the helm, and Antonio had big plans for the realtor…big plans.

Chapter 29

Antonio snugged the wires just a little tighter around Alfredo's body and signaled to his men to begin painting him with honey. Three buckets of honey. Three big sloppy paint brushes. Three men would get the job done right. This is what this devil deserves, thought Antonio, as he presided over the ceremony near the surfer's beach. Tie him to a tree and let him rot.

The thin wires, wrapped around a huge palm tree, then around Alfredo's body nearly every inch or so, were already cutting into his skin, already causing the areas around his armpit and ankles to swell and turn blue.

Alfredo noticed his body was facing south, so if he made it through the night, the afternoon sun would surely finish off the job.

The following morning the town woke up a little late, feeling the effects of the three-day celebration. Another beautiful, tropical sunrise broke through the horizon, sprinkling the air with colorful, impressionistic colors. A few people rolled in the surf, fully clothed—leftovers from the night before, the final night of the Esmeralda Days celebration.

They would be taking another day off, something the natives referred to as a "Puente" or bridge, meaning if they had a three day weekend, many would take four days off, a day before in preparation for the holiday. The beach was still littered with rum and coke bottles, since even those who would be cleaning up the holiday mess were still sleeping.

Alfredo, who sure enough, had made it through the night without incident, noticed all three of his guards, the men who had painted him with honey, were asleep in the sand next to him. And then, he heard them before he saw them: sniffling, squeaking and shrieking searching for the source of the mix of sweat and honey.

"Hey hombres. Wake up," Alfredo yelled, seeing a huge line of hungry looking Jefe rats coming in his direction.

They were starting to circle him, moving slow, eyeing him with their big gray eyes.

"Hombres," a little more urgently this time. The three guards opened their eyes, saw the rats and wondered out loud, "What took them so long?"

"Maybe they needed his body heat to warm things up a bit. Maybe they were tired like the rest of us...It has been a rather long celebration, que no?"

"Maybe they weren't hungry. Oh, they look hungry now," the third man said, just a little louder to be sure that Alfredo heard him.

He heard him all right. He heard every word, every breath they had taken. And he didn't like what he heard. These men weren't going to stop the rats.

Nando had flown through the air and just before impact pulled his handcuffed arms under his feet and tucked into a little ball, just like when he rolled down his hill, and landed with a thud. He felt like he was hitting cement, not water. Still, once the initial impact was over, he gathered his wits, took a big breath and dove as far as he could, trying to stay out of sight of the hovering metal.

He had pulled it off. He had embraced the negative powers of the mainland, just like the turtles gods had urged him to do, and he had taken the hot lead, the flying metal and survived. All his years of training had allowed him to follow the wisdom of the turtles and not resist. The special honey he had taken from the sacred temples had certainly worked.

Now, as he landed on his black sand beach a surprised Martin met him. Martin had truly thought Nando wouldn't survive, being handcuffed and all. And now, here stood the small, wiry and very tough Indian, full of smiles.

"Can you get these off," Nando moaned, jangling his handcuffs.

"Yes. Let's head into town and take care of it."

On the way in Martin told Nando how he had been searching all morning for a simple answer to a straightforward question. What kind of leatherback turtle had a small bee sized emerald spot on its belly.

They had taped into many of the big libraries of the United States and Mexico; chatted with three different turtle experts, one in Mexico, one in the U.S. and one in Ecuador. With all three they had asked a list of questions, Martin had suggested this, so they wouldn't give away their secret.

The unequivocal answer, by all the experts, was, no there wasn't a leatherback, or any sea going turtle for that matter, that had an emerald spot of its belly.

"They really are different my friend," Nando said.

"That's it," Martin cooed. "It really is a lost breed. We win," Martin said, shaking his head in excitement.

The ramifications were enormous. During the whole morning, while waiting for answers from various sources, they had already discussed their plan to broadcast to the world that Esmeralda, did indeed have a never before discovered breed of turtle—the Emerald Belly.

"This, " Martin said, jumping up and stretching his aching body, "will surely save the Black Sands Beach." He'd been on the island for only a short while, but it had changed him, he thought, scratching at his goatee.

Chapter 30

That night Martin sat on Gorde's porch, drinking tequila and sangrita with a flourish, and celebrating their victory. They had come a long way since that first day, when Martin, drunk and hot, had jumped on his surfboard and floated around to the black sands beach. And, like the islander's said, especially the women on the island, everything had worked itself out. In fact, everything was downright perfect.

The two men stayed up all night, drinking and celebrating and whooping it up. After all, they had won. A small green bug, about the size of a corn kernel, crawled by in the early morning darkness. Martin had named these little green illuminating machines "Lady Esmeraldas." The first night he had seen them he had seen a dead bug that was still putting out a bright green light. Martin had pondered what mechanism had allowed for the bug to continue glowing. He put it in a jar and a week later, forgetting about his little experiment, he accidentally stumbled upon the jar, on his porch, in the dark, with the green light still glowing inside the jar, giving it a green jack o' lantern glow.

Another mystery from the island, Martin had thought. How many more undiscovered treasures were on this primitive island. The bees, they were certainly unique. Of course, the turtles. The Lady Esmeralda bugs. What else? The cure for cancer? Aids. Who knew?

And now, sitting on the porch with Gorde, feeling the effects of his strong tequila, they continued the celebration.

"We showed 'em," Gorde slurred with a smile.

"Ya," Martin agreed. "I'm still in awe that they backed down."

As they tinked glasses for the 84th time Gorde's wife Vicki stuck her head in and yelled, "Hey you two. We need your help."

"Carina," Gorde moaned, "can't you see we're busy."

"They have Alfredo under wire."

When Gorde heard the word wire, he was up. "Where?"

"Surfer's Beach," Vicki glumly revealed, shaking her head back and forth.

Gorde waved for Martin to follow and he did, asking, "What's under wire?"

"We have a tradition around here, Gorde said. It's a pretty ugly one at that. When someone wrongs the village, in a way that is a disgrace, they are put under wire. This village has been hurt and now, they're doing some damage to the mainlander who caused it. Alfredo. It's gonna be ugly my friend. It's really not a good thing, revenge."

And that's all he would say, letting the image of the dehydrated yet swollen Alfredo, still wired to the palm tree, do the talking for him.

"My God," Martin involuntarily whispered when he saw the wired mess of flesh that used to be referred to as Alfredo.

"What happened? Is he still alive?"

"Good question," Gorde replied, "Unfortunately for him. I think so."

Gorde muttered under his breath as he clipped the first of many wires away from the ex-realtor. As he clipped away, it become apparent that some of the wire parts were imbedded in Alfredo's skin and weren't coming out. Alfredo's left eye opened and he whispered, "shoot me" in a soft, desperate voice.

Gorde thought about the option and knew that it would probably be the most humane approach to this man's problem, but he would have to stick to tradition. It was a tradition that even Alfredo knew well. And that was why he had pleaded for the bullet.

"Please," Alfredo murmured through lips coated with dried blood.

Gorde could see that the guards had left Alfredo alone with the Jefe rats and they had taken a few chunks out of Alfred's skin and, disliking the rancid taste of his meat, left him alone to die in the sun. The heat, unfortunately, hadn't completed the job.

Now, with most of the wire out, Gorde, knowing this man was in for a lot of pain and suffering, offered him a tequila and when Alfredo blinked his eyes yes, Gorde poured a generous dose into the culprit's mouth. Then, hoping he wouldn't have to baby-sit this wired pile of flesh for too long, he carried Alfredo Lopez Ramos, with his gold bracelets stuck to his puffed skin, down to the water, gently laid him into the clear, blue and salty pacific and walked away.

Alfredo let out a yell that would have drowned out a 747 jet; a yell that would have broken glass from Esmeralda to China if it had been one octave higher. A yell that, if you listened carefully, could probably be heard way on the other side of the island, in Hermana, and probably, even in the deepest reaches of Nando's cave. As Alfredo's scream rang out over the village. As his high pitched death-defying yell rang in the ears of each and every resident of the village, Stan Lovejoy, lying in his hammock, opened a message marked urgent from Mexico City.

In fact, it was from the President of Mexico, addressed to the mayor of Esmeralda (Stan wondered how they had even found out that he was now the official acting mayor).

"I guess good news travels fast," he had joked.

The note, in short, said that the President of Mexico wanted to donate money for the new turtle reserve and later this year, when the reserve was finished, visit the fair island of Esmeralda and have a ceremony dedicating the new reserve.

Stan stood up from his hammock, both legs strong and sure, looked out over his domain. He saw man o' rays jumping out of the water, playing their strange game of hide and seek. He listened to the sound of the blackbirds, singing their peculiarly high-pitched tropical love songs, and he shook his head, smiled a wry smile and whispered to himself, "When will they ever learn?"

7